JORDAN'S CROSSING

Jack Denton is just another travel-stained wanderer when he fetches up in the town of Jordan's Crossing. There he finds a young widow, Marion Fowler, being terrorized by three men in her store, and kicks them out. But then the stakes are raised when her six-year-old son is kidnapped, and she receives a note telling her to leave the key to the store on her step. Why is there so much interest in the business — and what cost will Denton have to pay for solving the mystery and finding Marion's son?

ETHAN HARKER

JORDAN'S CROSSING

Complete and Unabridged

LINFORD
Leicester

First published in Great Britain in 2016 by
Robert Hale
an imprint of The Crowood Press
Wiltshire

First Linford Edition
published 2018
by arrangement with
The Crowood Press
Wiltshire

A catalogue record for this book is available
from the British Library.

ISBN 978–1–4448–3823–7

Published by
F. A. Thorpe (Publishing)
Anstey, Leicestershire

Set by Words & Graphics Ltd.
Anstey, Leicestershire
Printed and bound in Great Britain by
T. J. International Ltd., Padstow, Cornwall

This book is printed on acid-free paper

1

It was coming on to dusk and Jack Denton thought to himself that unless he wished to spend another night sleeping beneath the stars he might be best advised to bestir himself a little. He had little notion how far Jordan's Crossing was, measured in miles, and so no idea either how much longer he would be on the trail before reaching the town.

In the event Denton had no cause to be anxious, because as he cantered the mare up the dusty track which led to the crest of a hill he found that when he reached the highest point there was the little town, spread out before him like a child's playthings. The little white church truly looked like a toy from up there, as did the saloon and hotel, which he could also see along the street from the church. It was a pretty little place, neat and compact, and Jack Denton hoped that he would find somewhere willing to offer him a bed for the next few nights. He set the horse trotting forward and made his way down towards Jordan's Crossing.

Jordan's Crossing was, by all accounts, a peaceful town, full of law-abiding people who simply got on quietly with their lives. It was hearing this that had caused Denton to head in its direction; he had had enough excitement in his life already to last him for a good long while. His aim now was to take stock a little and perhaps even consider settling down for a spell.

First things first though, and before hunting out a bed for the night he thought he might buy a loaf of bread and maybe a hunk of cheese to go with it. Denton hadn't eaten since breaking his fast that morning and suddenly felt ravenously hungry. Opposite the church was a general store, a creosoted, one-storey, clapboard building, which looked like it might provide vittles for a hungry traveller. He dismounted, looped the reins loosely round the hitching rail and went into the store.

It was gloomy inside, although apparently not yet dark enough for anybody to think of lighting a lamp. Denton could see three shadowy figures at the back of the place, standing at the long wooden counter. One of these customers, for so he took them to be, was talking in a soft but ugly voice. This was a little surprising; it sounded more like some disputation in a bar-room than a routine mercantile transaction in a store. Denton caught the tail end of what was evidently some kind of argument, for he heard one of the men say:

'You don't want to get crosswise to me, I'm telling you. You hear what I say now?'

Since the end of the War Between the States Jack Denton had had enough trouble to last him his whole life, and he certainly did not feel the need to go hunting out any more. Whatever was going on in that store was no affair of his, so he turned, meaning to slip out quietly. Then he heard the reply to the vaguely menacing question that had just been posed. A woman said in a low and frightened tone:

'I hear what you say, all right.'

Cursing himself for not having left at once, Denton turned round and walked towards the back of the store. Not mixing himself up with another man's quarrel was one thing; ignoring a woman being bullied was something else again. Like as not it was some foolishness between husband and wife and they would both turn on him in a fury when he intervened, but it wouldn't sit right with him if he didn't at least check that this woman required no assistance.

As he crossed the floor of the store Denton's eyes adjusted themselves to the darkness. He saw that three men were leaning at the counter, facing a slender woman whom he took to be the proprietor of the store. He walked as soft-footed as a cat when he'd a mind to and none of the three men heard his approach. The first that they were aware of the presence of another party was when Denton cleared his throat and enquired diffidently:

'Everything all right, ma'am?'

He saw her face flood with relief as he spoke and knew instinctively that this was no common or garden domestic dispute, but a horse of another colour entirely. There was something unpleasant going on here and Jack Denton resolved then and there that he would straighten the matter out. He was not in general one for poking his snout into other folk's business, but neither was he about to walk away from the sight of three men apparently threatening a lone woman.

'You know what's best for you, pilgrim, you'll just turn around an' walk out that door,' said one of the three men. 'Else you're apt to find you've bit off more'n you can chew.'

'That so?' said Denton pleasantly. 'Fact is, I never was right good at doin' what's best for me. Bad habit, I'll allow.' He spoke past the men, directly to the woman behind the counter: 'Hope I'm not interfering none where I ain't wanted, but looks to me like these boys are troublin' you. That how things stand?'

'Oh, please help me. I don't know what they're after. They say I got to give up my store.'

Before Denton could hold any further conversation with the woman the three men began moving towards him, in a way that suggested they were eager for him to make himself scarce, right this very minute. He raised his hands up as far as his shoulders, with the palms turned outward pacifically. 'Wait up now,' he said, 'I surely ain't seekin' for to fall out with you fellows.'

Whatever might be Jack Denton's wish to avoid falling out with anybody, the men whose business he had interrupted evidently had other views on the subject; they were giving every appearance of wanting at the very least to crowd him, and most likely intending to deliver a beating to a jasper they clearly regarded as an interfering busybody. The man who reached him first swung a meaty fist at Denton's head. It was a powerful blow which, had it made contact, might have knocked him flying.

He hadn't wanted any violence but since these characters seemed so determined Denton thought that he might as well oblige them. Knocking aside the fist with a sharp chopping action of his right hand, he grasped the man's wrist and, using the momentum of the swing, kept it moving until he was able to twist the arm up behind the fellow's back. Then he gave a sharp shove and ran the man towards the counter, all the time keeping a firm hold of the arm. The other two were so taken aback by this unexpected development that they stood staring for a second.

When they got to the counter Denton rammed the man hard against it; then, still holding tight to his arm, he used his other hand to grab the fellow's hair and bang his head smartly on to the counter-top a couple of times. Having done this he twisted his victim round, so that he was between Denton and the other men. At the same time Denton drew his pistol, cocking it with his thumb as he brought it clear of the holster. Anybody were to start shooting at him now and they were apt to hit the man he was holding in front of him as a shield.

'I don't rightly know what you men are about,' Denton said, 'but I tell you now, I don't care for it. What say you two move real slow to that street door and walk through it? I'll follow on with this friend of your'n.'

Of course, much depended at this point on how much those other two valued the man Denton was holding in front of him. If he was no more than a casual acquaintance, then they might be disposed to commence shooting anyway and be damned to the other man's chances. As it was, they seemingly did not wish to see their companion killed, because with glowering looks that spoke of what they might wish to do to Jack Denton if he were at their mercy they turned slowly and walked to the door. Both made sure to keep their hands well away from their pistols.

Denton followed on and, as soon as the first two had left, gave the man whose arm he still gripped a mighty shove, sending him sprawling on to the boardwalk. He covered all three of the men with his own gun and they must surely have realized that he would be able to shoot any or all of them before they were able to draw.

'You fellows just walk clear down the road without turning round,' said Denton. 'I'll warrant I can kill all three of you 'fore you can draw down on me.' They could see from his eyes that this was no idle boast; they complied without further parley.

The thing that struck Marion Fowler, when she ran over the startling events in her mind later that day, was the sheer speed of the business. One moment the soft-spoken stranger was standing there quietly, like he was shy of interrupting a private conversation, and the next he had moved with dizzying rapidity and bested the three tough-looking men who had been trying to buffalo her into giving up her store.

The nearest comparison that she was able to make from her own experience was the memory of seeing a snake strike when she was a child. An inquisitive chipmunk had been busying itself, scuttling to and fro in the field behind her house. She had been watching the snake earlier; a fat and lethargic-looking reptile, which slithered idly through the scrubby grass. You would have thought that it was the least aggressive of creatures and had all the time in the world as it made its way across the dusty field.

Howsoever, the chipmunk had got

too close and the snake had reared up and then sunk its fangs in the rodent that was skittering around it. It had been so fast that had you blinked you would have missed it. That was what the ejection of the three men from the store had been like. Mrs Fowler guessed that they had been similarly surprised by the turn of events and the speed with which they had been compelled to leave.

After seeing that the men had really gone a fair way down the street, Denton went back into the store and took the precaution of slipping the catch on the door. He didn't want the three of them to come bursting back in with their guns blazing. He walked across to the counter.

'I hope you're not too shook up by all that, ma'am?' he said. Then he saw that her face was pale with shock and that she was shaking as if she had the ague. 'Lordy,' added Denton solicitously, 'you're tremblin' like an aspen leaf. You have a chair back there as you can set yourself down on?'

'I have. Thank you, you're very kind.'

'It's naught. Set down now and don't talk more than you will. Happen you might want to lean forward and rest your head down towards your lap. Helps somewhat if you're feelin' faint, or so I've found.'

The woman did as suggested and found that she did indeed feel better. After a few seconds she sat up straight again and said:

'My name's Marion Fowler and I'm more grateful than I can say for your help. I don't know what would have happened, else.'

'That's nothing; glad I could be of assistance. My name's Denton. Jack Denton. It's lucky I was passing.'

'I think I'll shut up for the day, Mr Denton. You've been very good. I thank you.'

There was a thoughtful look on Denton's face, but he hesitated to push himself forward. Nevertheless, he enquired tentatively.

'You live far from here, Miss Fowler?'

'It's Mrs. No, maybe a mile down the way. Why d'you ask?'

'Is your husband coming to walk you home?'

'I have no husband. He's dead,' she replied shortly.

'Well then, I don't reckon as you should set off just yet awhiles. Give those boys time to get clear would be my advice.'

'I see. Yes, I dare say you're right. I hadn't thought of that. I'm not used to this sort of thing, you know. We're so peaceful here that I can't quite believe what happened.'

Jack Denton's stomach was rumbling in protest and he realized that he was still starving hungry. Still, he could not simply walk off now. At the least he would have to see this woman safely to her home.

'I ain't being curious like,' he said, 'but what has happened? Who were those boys and what were they after?' Then, feeling that he might have overstepped the bounds of propriety, he added, 'Not that it's any affair of mine and please don't think as I'm pryin'.'

'I don't think any such thing, Mr Denton. You've been kindness itself and I haven't felt able to tell anybody of this. I'd like to talk about it.'

Denton gave a shy smile.

'Well then ma'am,' he said, 'I'm all ears, as the saying goes.'

'I guess it started about six months ago,' Mrs Fowler began, frowning slightly with the effort of remembering, 'When I got a letter from a firm of property agents up at the county seat. They wanted to take over the lease on this place. Offered me a right good price too.'

'Forgive me, I ain't precisely a man of business. You don't own this store?'

'No, my husband, God rest him, bought a ten-year lease on it the year before he died. That was three years back and so I have it for the next seven years. The letter offered me good money for surrendering the lease or transferring it to the company that wrote me.'

Denton rubbed his chin meditatively. 'So it was just a business proposal, is that the strength of it?'

'So I thought at the time, yes.'

'Like I say, I've not had a whole heap o' commercial dealings in my life, but those fellows I turfed out of here didn't strike me as being like most of the men of business I come across before.'

Marion Fowler shivered in the recollection of the men who had lately been in her store.

'I don't know what to make of it,' she said. 'I wrote back to the property company, declining their offer, and they upped it. I know what my late husband paid for the lease here and the men in the property company were offering more for just the remaining seven years than he paid for the thing in the first place. Something didn't sound right.

'Then, just before you walked in, those three men came in and told me that if I didn't give up the lease there would be trouble for me.'

It was getting dark and the woman stood up and lighted a lamp. As its warm light flooded the store she looked curiously at this stranger, so quiet and gentle on the outside and yet like a rattler when he was pushed.

She said, 'I'm sorry for involving you in my problems, Mr Denton.'

'You didn't involve me in nothing, ma'am. I'm my own boss. Tell me, could this be one of those rackets where men threaten trouble and then expect payment for backing off? What they call the protection game?'

She thought for a moment and then said slowly:

'I can't think that it was, you know. These men wanted me to take money. They didn't ask for anything from me, other than that I let somebody buy up the lease here.'

'It's a regular conundrum,' said Denton, 'and truth to tell, I can't make head nor tail of it. Will you let me walk you home?'

'Thank you.'

Marion Fowler locked up the store and Denton led his horse as the two of them walked along Main Street. When they reached a pretty little white-painted house on the edge of town, she said:

'You'll eat with us this evening, Mr Denton?'

'Us?'

'Me and my son. Davy's six and I'm sure he'd like to meet you. My sister lives next door and he stays with her during the day.'

The idea of eating was an appealing one, but he was reluctant to accept such an invitation, wondering if it would be precisely delicate to set at table with a lone woman in that way. Marion Fowler saw the indecision in his face and divined the reason for it.

'Come Mr Denton,' she said lightly, 'my son will prove an adequate chaperone. Please, I owe you some recognition for what you did.'

Denton smiled suddenly. 'I won't

deny that some food would come in right welcome, ma'am,' he said. 'Tell you the truth, I've not ate since daybreak.'

'Why, that settles it for certain sure. I can't let you leave hungry. Say you'll come in. Please. We so seldom have company.'

'I'm mighty obliged to you. Yes, I'll be pleased to set with you and your son.'

Margaret Hilton, who was Marion Fowler's sister, looked as though she was consumed with curiosity when they knocked on her door with a view to reclaiming young Davy.

'Why Marion,' she said archly, 'who's this handsome fellow?'

'Oh hush up, Margaret,' said her sister, flushing like a schoolgirl. 'This here's Mr Denton, who was kind enough to come to my aid today. I'll tell you about it tomorrow. Is that son of mine ready now?'

'Surely. Won't you come in while I get him ready?'

'No, just shoot him out as he is. I must be getting on.'

The meal was a pleasant, easy-going occasion and Jack Denton found the company of both Marion Fowler and her son Davy most agreeable. When it was ended he rose, thanked his hostess and announced his intention of leaving to find a bed for the night.

'You might try the hotel,' said Mrs Fowler. 'I happen to know that they're struggling somewhat and are always glad to let rooms out. Leastways, that'll do for this night. Are you fixing for to stay long in town?'

'I couldn't say,' replied Denton. 'It depends, I guess.'

'Well, I hope that I'll see you again before you leave. If you decide to go off, then be sure to drop by the store to bid farewell.'

'I'll be sure to do that, ma'am. I wish you both goodnight.'

As he strolled back to the centre of town to try his luck at the hotel Jack Denton's mind was racing. It had been a good long while since any woman had affected him as deeply as Marion Fowler had. When all was said and done he was most likely only passing through this place, so it would hardly be fair to set out a-courting of her. He'd an idea that she was the sort of woman who wouldn't be inclined towards some brief love affair and he didn't precisely aim to marry anybody just now.

The Metropolitan & Commercial Hotel, a grand name for a run-down little joint that was little better than a common lodging house, was only too delighted to offer him a room for the night. As he climbed into bed, Denton knew that whatever else chanced, he would be looking in on the store the next day.

2

When the War Between the States ended in 1865 Jack Denton had been twenty-five. He had been fighting for very nearly the whole of the previous four years and the arrival of peace left him strangely bereft. So used was he to bloodshed and battle that he scarcely knew what he would do next. One thing he did know for sure, though, was that he would not be going back to the smallholding in Kansas where he had been living with his wife and child. The memories would be too painful and he would be haunted by their imagined presence.

So it was that, as soon as the instrument of surrender had been signed at Appomattox Courthouse in April, Denton took off and roamed the Midwest, pursuing any number of varied and disparate occupations. These ranged from working as a deputy sheriff to rounding up cattle; from digging ditches to riding shotgun on a mail coach. Anything, rather than stay in one place for too long.

Lately though, he had had a hankering to settle down, at least for a month or two. He didn't want for money and even had some stashed away at a bank if he needed any extra. He'd heard that Jordan's Crossing was a nice, quiet little place and thought that he might spend some time there, gathering his thoughts and deciding what to do next.

⋆   ⋆   ⋆

The following morning Jack Denton was up early and, though he tried to pretend otherwise to himself, found that he was embarrassingly eager to call by the store to see Marion Fowler. After a light breakfast furnished by the hotel he walked out into a brilliantly fine May morning. As he did so he almost barged right into the fellow he

22

had manhandled the day before. The two men recognized each other immediately; both stopped dead in their tracks and stood staring, the one at the other.

It was a delicate situation, because had Denton himself been treated so roughly he would not have rested until he had wreaked vengeance upon whoever had had the temerity to lay hands upon him. He wondered if this man would feel the same. The silence stretched out, with neither of them saying a word. At length, desiring to bring matters to a point, Jack Denton said:

'Well friend, if you're wanting satisfaction, I'm altogether at your service. We can go somewhere private if you're shy o' settling things in the public highway.'

For a moment it looked as though the man might be about to take him up on his offer, but then he seemed to collect himself and, with a brief shake of his head, he walked straight past

Denton without a word, heading off along Main Street. Denton looked after him, with a puzzled and dissatisfied look on his face. If there was to be trouble he preferred to take it head on and have it out of the way. He made no doubt that that man would be coming after him before too long, but was for now too much engaged upon some more important business.

'I'd take oath as he's still thinking of that pretty little widow's store,' muttered Denton to himself. 'Well then, good luck to him. Like as not, our paths will cross again soon enough.'

Keen as he was to see and speak to Marion Fowler again, it struck Denton that it might look as though he were presuming a little were he just to march straight into the store, first thing in the morning. He would acquaint himself with the town first and then call in at the store in a casual way in the afternoon.

Just as he had been told, Jordan's Crossing was a peaceful place whose citizens were concerned only with tending to their own affairs and looking after their families. Everywhere he looked Denton saw signs of quiet industry and sober regard for the common good. It was refreshing to spend time in such a place. He had a haircut and shave, and the barber, in the course of conversation, confirmed Denton's view of the town.

'No siree, nothin' much happens in these here parts. Last bit of excitement we had around here was the last year o' the late war, when we was all drove out of our own town, if you can believe it.'

'I believe you. There was some terrible things done at that time.'

'Ah, I'm guessing you was a soldier?'

'That I was,' said Denton shortly, not wishing to expand on the topic. 'You say you were driven from the town?'

'Yes, that's right. It was only for three days, mind, but that was just about long enough for all the folk here to be sleeping rough, up in the hills, some with little 'uns and all.'

'What happened?'

'Well now,' said the barber as he applied lather to Denton's neck and chin, 'the war didn't much affect us 'til that day. Then a troop of Rebels fetched up. Wagons, carts, artillery, the whole caboodle. Gave us two hours to clear out of our own town, if you don't mind! Any as refused, they said, would be shot. Commandeered our houses and I don't know what all else.'

'So what happened next?' asked Denton patiently. 'Did they cause any damage?'

'No, not overmuch. Just what their spurs did to upholstery and the odd cigar burn. Scarcely nothing to speak of. Then they just upped and left.'

'You know what they were doing here?'

'No, 'cause they no sooner left town than they was ambushed by Federal cavalry. Nigh on wiped out every one o' them greycoats. Don't know to this day what they were doing here.'

Feeling more like a human being and

less like a wild beast that has been roaming the plains, Jack Denton paid the barber for his services and included a generous tip. It surely made a heap of difference to a man, being clean-shaven and with his hair neatly trimmed. Maybe he'd look a little more respectable when he went calling at Mrs Fowler's store that afternoon.

So full of such thoughts was he that Denton was taken quite by surprise when, as he left the barber's shop, a man standing right by the door reached down and plucked Denton's pistol from its holster. He turned angrily, meaning to ask the man what he thought he was about, when a stunning blow, coming from the other side of the doorway, struck his head. As he fell face forward, toppling from the boardwalk, he lost his footing entirely and landed in the dirt of the roadway. Denton had just enough time to figure out that there must have been men stationed on either side of the door to the barber's shop, just waiting for him to emerge.

Although the sudden assault had taken him altogether by surprise, Denton's reactions were quick enough. He bounced once in the dust and then, like a cat, whirled round and was back on his feet, facing the three men who had jumped him. It came as no surprise to find that they were the self-same men whom he had thrown out of Marion Fowler's store the day before.

'Three on one?' Denton said. 'You call that a fair fight?'

'You managed well enough yesterday,' said one of the men. 'You'd o' done better to stick your nose in a hornet's nest than mix it with us.'

Although he had not the least intention of backing down there was no percentage in letting the men, who had now stepped down from the boardwalk, realize that. Denton moved back slowly.

'You was pickin' on a woman,' he said. 'What d'you expect me to do?'

'Expect you to mind your own damned business,' replied one of the men, coming closer and swinging his foot at Denton. 'Not gettin' yourself tangled up in things as don't concern you.'

Jack Denton's past experiences had led him to conclude that fighting and talking were two very different activities and best kept separate. Chatting while trying to fight was apt to distract one and lead to mishaps. He was given ample evidence that he was right about this when the fellow who had lashed out with his foot took another kick at him while he was offering Denton his advice about keeping his nose out of other folk's business.

Denton grabbed the man's foot and then gave it a sharp and expert twist, bringing the fellow to the ground. Without waiting any longer he launched himself against another of his opponents, driving his fist into the man's throat. As he turned to deal with the third of them a two-pound chunk of iron slammed into the side of Jack Denton's head. This was repeated a couple of times, as the man on whom he'd turned his back began pistol-whipping Denton to the ground. Then the other two joined in, kicking him as he went down, then leaning over to rain punches upon him. He wondered if they were after beating him to death.

As he curled up to protect his face from the onslaught, Denton heard a voice saying:

'All right then, just you boys break it up now. What do'you mean by it, brawling in the gutter like kids?'

The attack ceased and Denton got to his feet, finding to his relief that he appeared to be suffering from nothing worse than a few bruises. Standing twenty feet away was a man in late middle age. His hair was iron grey and he had a moustache to match. The most important thing that Denton noticed was that this individual was cradling a sawn-off scattergun in his arms, the weapon being aimed generally at both him and the three men who had ambushed him.

'Well,' said the old fellow who was

drawing down on the four men who had been fighting, 'I'm still waiting. I don't ask questions for the sake of my health, nor nothing like it. What's going on? 'Case you boys don't know it, my name's Quinn and I'm the sheriff hereabouts. Well? Cat got your tongues?'

'We was just foolin' about, Sheriff,' said Denton easily. 'No harm meant, I'm sure. Sorry to have caused you any trouble.'

Quinn narrowed his eyes suspiciously.

'That a fact?' he said. 'Sure didn't look like play fighting. I'd o' said that those men were set fair to kill you.'

'Ah, we're friends really. Like I say, it was just foolishness. We're sorry.' He turned to the men who just lately had been bludgeoning him, saying, 'Ain't that right, boys?'

'Sure,' replied the man who had pistol-whipped Denton to the ground. 'We wouldn't o' dreamt o' hurtin' this fellow. Why, he's a real friend of ours.'

None of the three men who had been trying to injure, maybe even kill him, evinced the least surprise at Jack Denton's efforts to give the sheriff the brush-off. Truth to tell, they would have been taken aback had he complained to Quinn about the unprovoked attack that they had launched. They calculated, quite correctly, that Denton was like them, in that he preferred to settle matters man to man rather than involving the law in such things.

Sheriff Quinn was far from satisfied. His office was just across the way from the barbershop and he had had a perfect view of the whole episode, watching as one man was jumped by three as he came out after having a shave. Quinn knew damned well that more was going on than a bit of fun.

'I'm more'n half-minded to run all four of you in for disorderly conduct,' he said. 'You ain't from round here, are you? Let me tell you, this here's a nice, peaceful town and s'long as I'm the law, that's how it'll stay.'

The men to whom he was talking stood quietly, trying to look as meek and inoffensive as lambs. The effect was anything but convincing and at last Quinn said:

'Ah, get out o' my sight, the lot of you. Mark what I say, any more rough-housing like that in the street and I'll be locking people up and fining them a tidy sum into the bargain. Go on, off with you!'

As Quinn walked away Denton saw that the barber had come out of his shop and was beckoning him over. When he reached him, the man said:

'Lookee here, I retrieved your gun. That man as took it just let it fall to the boardwalk.' He handed the pistol to Denton, who thanked him and then went off to the saloon.

The optimistically named Royal Flush was the only bar in Jordan's Crossing. When he walked through the batwing doors it was clear that the saloon was not open for business. An old man was sweeping the floor and all the chairs had been set on the tables to facilitate this operation. Without looking round the oldster said:

'Ain't open yet. Come back in an hour or so.'

'I'm not looking for a drink. I was hoping to find information.'

The man stopped sweeping and shot Denton a suspicious look.

'That's a dangerous commodity and no mistake,' he said. 'What sort of information you after?'

The owner of the Royal Flush was sixty-three years old and as shrewd and careful a man as you could hope to meet anywhere in the state. Despite his advanced years, wherever there was a job of work to be done in the bar-room he would do it himself if he could, sooner than pay another to undertake the task.

He had already marked the arrival in town of the three strangers and had heard indirectly that they claimed some interest in the little store being run by the Widow Fowler. Now here was

34

another out-of-towner, looking for information. The saloon keeper wasn't a gambling man, but he would be prepared to wager a hundred dollars that the information being sought had some reference to the general store down the street a ways. He was thoroughly enchanted with his own perspicacity when the young man standing there asked:

'Can you tell me anything 'bout that store, down the way? The general store run by a lady called Marion Fowler?'

'What you want to know?'

'What can you tell me?'

'Fellow called Bergen owned the lot. Built the store three, maybe four years back. Just after the war. Marion Fowler's husband as was, Pete, he bought the lease on the place and Marion Fowler's run it since. No secrets there, same as everybody knows.'

'Nothin' else?'

'Not a damned thing. Mind telling me what all the interest is in that store? You ain't the first to enquire this week, but I'm guessing you know that already.'

'You mean three men been askin' about it too?'

'That's right. Happen you're a friend o' theirs?'

'Not hardly. Well, thanks for your help.'

When Denton was a boy his grandmother had been a powerful strong woman for Scripture. The old lady had endeavoured by various methods to persuade her scapegrace grandson to share her enthusiasm for the word of the Lord, but somehow he'd never taken to religion. One or two sayings from the Good Book had stuck in his memory though, including one passage which held that: *He that passeth by and meddleth with strife not belonging to him, is like one that taketh a dog by the ears.*

Which, said Jack Denton to himself as he left the Royal Flush, is pretty much what I've been about since first I set foot in this town yesterday. I've been meddling in some quarrel that has nothing to do with me and the result is pretty much the same as though I'd grabbed some stray dog by the ears. I've got myself bitten. Question is, can I leave it alone now or do I carry on mixing myself in with somebody else's business?

After killing time in various ways and checking that his horse was being well tended at the livery stable and so on, Denton managed to avoid dropping by the store until about two that afternoon. Mrs Fowler was polite and pleased to see him, but did not, as he had secretly hoped she might, invite him to visit her home again. Feeling vaguely dissatisfied and a little sad, Denton left the store and decided to burn off some energy by going for a good long walk in the hills that surrounded Jordan's Crossing.

It was coming on dark by the time that Denton got back to town and he felt all the better for his exertions. He had been unable to stop thinking about

Marion Fowler all afternoon, which was irksome. It had been a long while since a woman had caught his attention in this way and it was an unfamiliar and not wholly comfortable feeling. He wandered disconsolately back to the hotel where he was staying and ordered a meal, which he then sat eating moodily alone.

While he was tucking into his steak Denton thought that there would be no harm in trying to get to know Mrs Fowler a little better. He resolved to ask her if she and her boy would care to go for a picnic this coming Sunday. The worst that she could say would be no and at least he might gain some idea of whether she could have any interest in a restless saddle bum such as him. It wasn't likely, he was forced to allow, but you never could tell.

After he'd eaten Denton still felt restless and thought to stretch his legs again, if only for a walk around town. It was dark now and, being a weekday, there weren't many people out and about. He strolled down Main Street, past the general store. As he went by he saw from the corner of his eye the faintest flicker of light from the front window. The shutters were down and it was only because he happened to be in the right position at the right time that he saw it.

He knew at once that without any shadow of a doubt, somebody was inside the store with a lantern. More than that, the lamp must be shielded, so that it shed but a little light. Denton wondered for a moment if his eyes had deceived him, so he turned and walked past the building once more, this time focusing his eyes on the cracks between the shutters of the windows. Sure enough, he saw again the glimmer of a guarded light.

Try as he might, Jack Denton could think of no reason why Marion Fowler should be tiptoeing around her own store at night with a shaded lantern. He'd never heard of any honest person finding a need for such a thing in a store at night and the natural corollary of this thought was that somebody was up to no good. Even leaving the widow out of his equations, Denton was mightily intrigued by the goings-on regarding that store. If Marion Fowler was telling the truth, and he had no reason in the world to doubt that she was, then that store of hers contained nothing of any particular value, other than the pots and pans, broomsticks and lamp oil that she stocked for sale. There was something queer going on and he was determined to get to the bottom of it.

It didn't occur to Denton for one moment to fetch the sheriff and report what he had seen. Since whatever was going on most likely involved those men who had jumped him earlier that day, this was a personal affair between him and them. Looking after Mrs Fowler's interests might be playing a certain role in things, but the plain fact was that he had unfinished business with the three men who had tried to injure him and

Denton owed it to himself to settle up with them. It wouldn't do for folk to think that they could just kick him around like some mangy dog and then get away with it scot free.

He slid the Colt Navy from where it nestled at his hip and cocked it all in the same fluid motion. Then he moved round to the side of the building. This led him to a broad alleyway running behind the buildings that fronted Main Street.

As soon as he reached the alleyway Denton could see that he was on the right track, because a man was standing in the shadows, at about the position where Denton thought the store might be. At a guess he assumed that this fellow had probably been posted as lookout and that, unless he, Denton, was greatly mistaken, his two partners would be poking around inside Marion Fowler's store, searching for the Lord knew what.

As he walked slowly down the alley towards the man, three things happened in quick succession. The first was that the moon suddenly emerged from behind the clouds, flooding the narrow space between the buildings as dramatically as if somebody had lit the limelight in a theatre.

A moment later the man standing at the back of the store turned in Denton's direction; the two men instantly recognized each other. Denton saw the very fellow whom he had been obliged to throw out of the store on the day he arrived in Jordan's Crossing.

The third thing that occurred was that the man he was approaching drew a gun and began firing at Denton, with the evident intention of putting an end to his life.

3

In a way, having the man start shooting in this way was a relief, because it brought matters to a head and meant that Denton could act rather than just bandy words. It had been clear to him since first he had tackled this fellow that there would be a reckoning; this was it.

The first two shots went whistling past Denton; the man firing at him was clearly taken by surprise and had drawn and fired by reflex. After those first two ranging shots though, it would be a racing certainty that the next would find its billet, which would most likely be in Jack Denton's heart. He dived behind a galvanized steel trash can and sat perfectly still. By a mercy the moon slipped back behind a cloud, casting the area into shadow once more. In the distance dogs had begun barking and one or two windows had been thrown up with a rattle, as folk peered out into the night to see what the devil was going on.

Denton slid his own pistol from its holster and cocked it. Although he was in a great hurry to get away from the alley before any inquisitive person came poking his nose into the place in an effort to find out what was going on, Denton knew that his best bet was to remain still and quiet. With any luck the man who had shot at him would come to the conclusion that one of his balls had hit the mark and that the man he had the grievance with was lying dead in the mud.

So it proved, because he heard soft and cautious footsteps approaching. Then a head appeared over the top of the trash can, as the man who had tried to kill him peeped over to see if he had succeeded in his endeavours.

'Hidy!' said Denton and fired point blank between the fellow's eyes, killing him on the spot. Then, with no more ado, he stood up, holstered his piece and walked briskly back down the alley, making his way to Main Street. In two minutes he was back at the hotel.

Once back in his room Denton moved swiftly. He took out his pistol, tapped out the wedge holding the barrel in place and removed it. Then he immersed the hexagonal tube in his wash basin and swirled it around a little. Leaving it to soak, he reloaded the chamber that had been fired, then took the barrel out of the basin and dried it on the towel. He squinted down it and saw that the inside was still sopping wet. This he remedied by tearing a piece off the towel and poking it down the interior of the barrel as far as it would go. He repeated the procedure at the other end, then reassembled the weapon.

Denton went to the window, threw it open and listened. In the distance he could hear men calling to each other. He'd an idea that the discharging of firearms at night was not a common event in this town and that shooting after dark was likely to be the subject of prompt investigation by Sheriff Quinn and his assistants. For all that Jordan's Crossing was so sleepy and quiet, he felt that Quinn was well up to the mark and that he was not a man to pass lightly over any gunplay in his town.

There was a man who was sharp as a lancet; the sheriff was, thought Denton, probably responsible in great measure for the tranquillity that reigned in his town. At a guess, he would say that Quinn would be very quick to blame outsiders for any disturbance in the smooth running of Jordan's Crossing; he probably kept a watch on any newcomers, to see that they behaved themselves.

So it proved, for not half an hour after he had returned to his room at the hotel Denton heard footsteps on the stairs and there came an imperious rapping on the door. Somebody said sharply:

'Open up! This is the law.'

It came as no great surprise to Jack Denton when he unbolted and opened his door to find Sheriff Quinn standing there, flanked by two grim-looking men. Without waiting for an invitation to enter, Quinn and his companions walked into the room and looked around.

'To what do I owe this unexpected pleasure?' enquired Denton courteously. 'Was you looking for anything in especial or just browsing?'

'Do not get smart with me,' said Quinn, in a tone that suggested he was not fooling. 'You're suspicioned for a murder which took place not an hour since.'

'Who do you say I killed?'

'Fellow you were brawling with earlier this day. Him as you said was your friend. Remember?'

'Sure. He's dead, you say? Well, I'm surely grieved to hear it.'

'Take out your pistol and hand it me,' said the sheriff, 'but real slow, you understand? Use your left hand to do it.'

As Denton complied with Quinn's instructions the two men whom he took to be deputies watched him closely. Denton had no doubt at all that if he showed any signs of aggressive intent, or even moved too fast, these men would surely draw and shoot him on the spot. He handed the pistol, hilt first, to the sheriff, who took it and held it at once to his nose, sniffing delicately, almost as though he were savouring the bouquet of some fine wine.

'Hmmm, it don't smell like it's been fired lately,' conceded Sheriff Quinn, never once taking his eyes from Denton's face. 'You got any other weapon?'

'No, but feel free to search.'

While the sheriff stood watching Denton the other two men went through the room methodically, looking for anything that might prove incriminating. They found nothing.

'I ain't satisfied, I'll tell you that for

nothing, Mr — ?'

'Denton, Jack Denton.'

'You ain't a-planning for to leave our town in any great hurry, I suppose?'

'Not a bit of it. You seemingly set a close watch upon strangers.'

'That I do,' said Quinn, 'and you see why. It's been nigh on two years since we've had a shooting here and that last was by an outsider, too.'

'You speak to the fellow's friends?' asked Denton helpfully. 'Maybe they could shed light on this business.'

'Don't fox with me, son. You think I didn't go looking for them as well? They lit out almost as soon as the shots were fired. Didn't even go back to the Royal Flush to settle the bill.'

'Well, there you are. Seems to me like you'd be better off chasing after them and asking what's what.'

'Don't try and teach me my job. I might want to speak to you tomorrow. I took the liberty of impounding your saddle from the livery stable. You can have it back when I'm satisfied you had no part in this.'

'Lordy,' said Denton, partly irritated and partly admiring, 'but you don't waste any time!'

'It's how I keep this town so peaceful, Denton. By setting a watch on ragamuffins and drifters such as your own self. I'll bid you good night.'

After Quinn left Jack Denton breathed a sigh of relief. He might technically have been defending himself against a murderous assault by the man he had killed, making the homicide justifiable, but there would only have been his word for that. His neck had been in peril and, if he hadn't thought to remove the smell of burnt powder as soon as could be, it was altogether possible that he might have hanged for the night's work.

Although he was pleased, not unnaturally, to have evaded the consequences of killing a man, Denton was none the less disturbed by the evening's events. Obviously, there was something very strange going on about that store of Marion Fowler's. What it might be he had not the least notion and there seemed little point in fretting over it now. Instead, he turned down the lamp and prepared for his bed.

Quinn had said nothing about where the body had been found, but Denton guessed that there would be a deal of gossip about the subject the next day. Shootings of that sort were not, from what the sheriff had told him, a regular feature of the town. Just as soon as he heard from some other source that the corpse had been found back of the store, then he would have an excuse to pay a visit and try to unravel the mystery.

The next day news was all over town about the shoot-out. There had been no excitement like it for the better part of two years and it was the theme of universal conversation. Best of all was where the victim of the murder wasn't even from Jordan's Crossing. He was just some fellow who had washed up in town a few days ago and was now lying on a trestle-table at back of the saloon, until Sheriff Quinn decided that he wished to see the corpse under ground. The fact that the dead man's two partners had upped sticks and left was another good point, because it meant that nobody in the town was like to be called to account for the death.

At breakfast Denton heard enough of the case to decide that he was not likely to make himself a suspect by displaying information which could only have been known by the murderer. Everybody had a theory on the motivation of the men who had killed their friend behind the stores on Main Street. That it was the two missing people who were responsible for the murder seemed beyond all reasonable doubt. After all, why else would they have vanished so promptly?

After taking a walk up and down the street a couple of times it seemed to Denton that he might reasonably drop by the store and ask after Mrs Fowler. As soon as he walked in the place the first person he saw was Sheriff Quinn.

'Oh, Mr Denton,' Marion Fowler said, 'I'm so pleased to see you. You heard, I suppose, what happened here last night?'

'You two know each other?' asked Quinn. 'How's that?'

'Why, Mr Denton was kind enough to help me out when I had some trouble on Tuesday.'

'Go on,' said Quinn. 'That was right nice of him. Care to tell me what this trouble consisted of?'

After he had heard the story of Denton throwing the three men out of the store, Sheriff Quinn turned to him.

'I dare say I'd be right in thinking that those were the same three men you were fighting with yesterday?' he suggested.

'It may be so.' said Denton noncommittally.

'Don't fool around. Were they the same men?'

'Yes, that's right.'

'Oh, Mr Denton, you never said

aught of this. I'm so sorry for getting you embroiled in this business.'

'It's nothing ma'am, I do assure you.'

'This is all real nice and cosy,' Quinn said, 'but it ain't what I'd call business. Somebody broke in here last night and the upshot was that there was a murder. I'm hopeful that Mrs Fowler here can help, see if she knows the dead man.'

'You can't ask a lady to look at a corpse,' said Denton, outraged. 'It's not to be thought of. I can identify the body well enough.'

'You can come as well, not instead of,' said the sheriff flatly. 'I know Mrs Fowler and she's a reliable witness. I'd take her word over yours. Only yesterday you were tellin' me as those men were by way of being old friends of yours; you recall that?'

'It's all right, Mr Denton,' said Marion Fowler. 'I don't mind helping out the sheriff. But I'm glad you'll be coming along of me.'

Sheriff Quinn snorted. 'Happen you know your own business best, Mrs

Fowler,' he said, 'but you might take care with the company you keep.'

Why the owner of the Royal Flush had allowed the sheriff to dump a dead body in his storeroom Denton never heard. He guessed that the fellow owed Quinn a favour. At any rate, there on a battered old table rested the corpse, covered over with an old curtain. As they approached the table with its grim burden, Denton said quietly to the woman:

'You don't need to do this 'less you want.'

'I guess it's my duty,' she replied in a quivering voice. 'Leastways, that's what the sheriff would say.'

Without any ceremony Quinn whipped the faded cloth from the body and revealed Denton's handiwork for all to see. It was a dreadful sight because nobody had even troubled to close the man's eyes. In consequence he gave every appearance of staring up at the ceiling. His face bore a faintly puzzled look, as though he couldn't quite figure out how he'd got himself into this situation. The answer to this riddle was to be found in the neat round hole positioned right between the dead man's eyes.

'That's the man who was in the store, Tuesday,' said Marion Fowler, before her legs buckled slightly and she swayed against Denton.

'There, you happy now, damn you?' said Denton. 'See now, the lady's on the point o' fainting.'

'You keep a civil tongue in your head, mister. This here the man you saw in the store on the day in question?'

'Yes it is. Cover him up, for the Lord's sake.'

Sheriff Quinn consented to place the old curtain back over the corpse. Denton was furious, not merely with Quinn for putting the woman through such an ordeal, but with himself for being the root cause of the matter. Had he not shot the man Marion Fowler would not have been forced to view the body. Knowing that it was ultimately his own fault made Denton even angrier with the sheriff.

'If that's all,' he said, 'can I take Mrs Fowler back to her store?'

'You can. But you recollect what I told you last night? Make sure you're around if I want to speak to you. I don't want to have to hunt round for hours; you hear what I say?'

After the sight of that body Mrs Fowler needed to rest and recover herself. She couldn't face the store for the time being.

'You want that I look after it for this morning?' Denton asked.

'You mean run it for me? I couldn't take such a liberty, after you've been so kind.'

'It's no liberty. I kept a store before, I know how things go.'

'Would you really, though? Just for an hour or two. I feel all overcome after seeing that poor man.'

'Poor man? He was threatening you, you know.'

'Even so, he didn't deserve to die.

What a terrible thing to happen. Do you think that Mr Quinn is right and that it was his friends who killed him?'

'I couldn't say, I'm sure,' said Denton guiltily. 'We best let the law take charge o' such things. I'm sure the sheriff is able to track down the man who did this.'

The morning passed pleasantly enough. There was a constant stream of customers, although most only spent a dime or two. It was plain that they had really been attracted by news of the break-in and murder and were hoping to see some evidence of the thrilling events in the store. If so, then they were to be disappointed, because apart from the splintered window frame in the back room, there was no sign at all of what had happened the previous night.

When the stream of visitors slowed Denton took the opportunity to look round the store in between customers. He knew that there must be something here that people wanted so badly that they were prepared to go to a great deal of effort to secure it. What it might be, though, was quite beyond him. A quick look at the stock and the cashbox had told him that this was no little gold mine. Denton thought that it probably only just brought in enough money for Mrs Fowler and her son to live on. Unless she had another source of income, he guessed that it must be something of a tight squeeze to get by on what the store brought in.

Then again, maybe it wasn't the store itself that was the attraction. Could the land be worth a fortune or something? That didn't seem to be likely either. There were a couple of empty lots near by, and if anybody wished to build on Jordan's Crossing's Main Street they wouldn't need to terrorize a widow woman to do so, or break into her premises either. By midday, when Marion Fowler appeared, having recovered somewhat, Denton was no closer to solving the mystery than he had been to begin with.

As he was about to quit the store, leaving Mrs Fowler to tend it, it occurred to Denton that simply asking the question outright might not be a bad scheme.

'Mrs Fowler,' he said, 'pardon me for speaking plainly, but is there really no reason you can think of why anybody would want this place?'

'I've been purely racking my brains,' she replied, 'and I can't call anything to mind. You can see for yourself what it's worth. Or not worth, which is nearer to the mark. Why anybody would commit murder over this little shack I've no more notion than you.'

The woman's words had the ring of truth about them. There seemed no reason for her to lie and it looked as though, now those scamps had left town, they were never likely to learn the explanation for the events of the last few days. In this though, Denton was to be proved quite wrong. The first intimation he received that the business was not yet settled for good and all was when he encountered the woman whom he had understood to be Mrs Fowler's sister, in a highly distressed state.

After handing over the store to its rightful proprietor Jack Denton had taken a turn along Main Street as far as Marion Fowler's house. He had no particular object in mind, other than merely stretching his legs. As he reached the the house next to that occupied by Mrs Fowler and her little boy the front door opened and out came Margaret Hilton. Denton raised his hat.

'Good afternoon to you, ma'am,' he said.

As soon as she saw him the woman rushed down her path, saying:

'You're Marion's friend, ain't you? Thank God! I'm that distracted I don't know what to do!'

'What's wrong? Can I help at all?'

'Lord only knows. I must hurry to tell Marion what's to do, but I couldn't say how she'll take it.'

'Take what?' asked Denton. 'You can't go in this state, you'll pardon me saying. Let's go back now and set on your front step and you tell me what's goin' on.'

He led the all but hysterical woman back into her garden and persuaded her to be seated. Then Denton sat beside her and said:

'Now ma'am, what's to do?'

'It's Davy, Marion's boy. I look after him, you know. I left him playing out back and when I returned he wasn't there. There was only this, just resting on the step with a stone on it.'

She handed Denton a sheet of paper. There was a message scrawled on it in writing that looked as though it could have been that of either a child or a semi-literate and uneducated adult, with capital letters scattered randomly throughout the message. It said:

GO tO Sherrif and Boy DieS. PuT sign in WinDow of STore, saying

Closed for BuiuldinG Work and Lock Store. LeeAve Key Here tonIte. Boy Will be Sent baCk safe, In 3 Days.

After reading this strange missive, Denton looked up sharply.

'You've searched for the boy?' he queried. 'This ain't some prank?'

'I've hunted high and low. Thought it might be a joke, first off.'

'You told nobody?'

'No, I hardly have had time. I was going to see my sister down at the store.'

'That's a sound scheme. I'll come along of you. Where's your husband, ma'am?'

'He's away. He ain't expected back for best part of a fortnight.'

'You've no other male protector, you and your sister?'

'Nobody in town right now, no.'

'Well then,' Jack Denton said quietly, 'if I'm not pushing myself forward, happen the two of you will allow me to

step into the breach, so to speak. Just
'til your husband returns, you understand.'

4

When she fully apprehended the import of the note left at her sister's house, Marion Fowler fainted dead away, tumbling as though lifeless to the floor of her store. Denton moved swiftly to the door to secure it against entry and then helped revive the distraught woman by splashing a little cold water on her temples.

When she came round Mrs Fowler began moaning, saying: 'My God, what'll become o' my baby. We must tell Sheriff Quinn at once.'

'You set a posse after those boys,' said Denton in a hard voice, 'and they'll kill your son if it aids their escape. Tell Quinn and you're like to be the death o' the child.'

The reproachful looks that the two women shot him made Denton feel like a worthless and cruel fellow, but the case was too desperate to be dressed up in fancy language.

'The only hope is for one man to find where they are and deal with the thing neatly,' he said. 'Did you two ladies grow up in these parts?'

The sudden enquiry about their early lives left Marion Fowler and her sister staring at Denton as though he'd taken leave of his senses. He said patiently:

'Those men must be fixin' on coming back here for something to do with the store. That means that they can't be hiding out too far from town. I'm wondering if either of you knows anywhere as might fit the bill. Place where you'd be out of sight and snug.'

There was silence as both the women turned over what he was saying; then Margaret Hilton said:

'What about the gullies, Marion?'

'The gullies?' asked Denton quickly. 'What's that?'

Marion Fowler roused herself and said in a rush, as though she was seizing upon a chance to save her son:

'There's hills over to the west of town, limestone. They're all wore away by rain, and criss-crossed with gullies and little caves. We used to go up there sometimes as children.'

'How far are they?'

'Maybe three miles from here.'

'Anywhere else that might be somewhere that two men could hide?'

Marian Fowler and her sister shook their heads doubtfully. Denton seemed lost in thought and neither of them liked to interrupt him. After a minute, he said:

'I got no saddle, which means goin' by shank's pony. Maybe that's not such a bad thing, though. One man on foot'll be more likely to do the job than a dozen riders.'

'You have a plan, Mr Denton?' asked Mrs Fowler, looking at him with a sudden wild hope in her eyes.

'Shut up the store, Mrs Fowler. You and your sister get back home and I'll engage to do all that I can to bring back your son.'

Jack Denton escorted the two women back along Main Street to their houses. This was because he wished to make perfectly sure that they didn't speak to anybody, nor give the clue to anyone in the town that there was anything amiss. The only real hope was for a single man to take action. If those who had snatched the boy heard a crowd of galloping men bearing down on them, then the Lord knew what foolish thing they might do. The child's life would be worth nothing at all to them.

After getting directions to the gullies there seemed no purpose in delaying further. Three miles would take an hour or so, if it was in a straight course from the town. He'd have to hope that the men wouldn't have thought it worth standing sentry-go. If they saw him coming he was altogether lost. It was not the first time Jack Denton had undertaken a task of this kind and he was feeling that, with a little good fortune, he might be able to bring the boy back safely before nightfall.

Although his main motivation was the very right and proper one of setting out to save a helpless child from danger, Denton could not completely rid his mind of the thought of how grateful the boy's mother would be for his safe return. Then he felt ashamed of himself for such a base thought. Imagine rescuing a helpless, frightened child and then calculating on the advantages in some romantic adventure! He felt disgusted that he could even think in such a way.

To take his mind off such matters Denton began toying over the best way of approaching the problem. If he'd had time to plan ahead, he'd have equipped himself with a carbine or even just some fowling piece like a scattergun or something. Competent a shot as he was with his pistol, Denton had no illusions about the outcome if somebody sitting upon a piece of high ground had a rifle in his hand and saw him coming on. Why, he wouldn't stand a chance!

He'd been walking for a half-hour when he saw what could be the place of which he'd been told. The hillocks and undulations on the low hills ahead gleamed white here and there, which suggested the presence of limestone. Denton sat down behind a tree and gathered his thoughts. Despite the probable presence of men who would kill him as soon as look at him, the main thing on Denton's mind was the mystery of that damned store. There had already been one death, but that hadn't deterred these boys in any wise. They had simply reacted by committing the sort of crime that would get them lynched almost for a certainty if they were to be caught. Whatever they were after must be worth the hell of a lot to them.

Something else had been nagging away at the back of his mind; now, sitting there and reasoning things out quietly, he saw what it was. Mrs Fowler said that she had received letters from some property firm up at the county seat. This suggested that somebody with money and brains had designs on the store. Judging by that childish note, though, the men whom he was currently hunting were not overly burdened with intelligence or education. Were there two sets of men trying to get that store, or were the men he had already had some dealings with just part of a bigger operation?

Well, thought Denton, this wasn't business! He checked his pistol, making sure that each of the copper caps fitted over the nipples was straight and true. Now wasn't the time for a misfire, that was for sure. A thought struck him. All his life he had followed the 'rattlesnake code'. Did the end here justify abandoning that code and attacking those men unawares, should he have the good fortune to come across them? This was a bit of a poser and no mistake! He had been about to step out from behind the tree, but now he paused and considered the question.

Men cannot live altogether without

laws to govern their behaviour, even when there are no police or courts to enforce right conduct; in such cases codes will come into being to moderate the worst excesses and beastliness to which some men are given.

Such a set of rules was the rattlesnake code. It was not a written document and most of the men who lived by it had never even seen it set down in black and white. Nevertheless, even the blackest of villains paid at least lip-service to the rattlesnake code. Jack Denton had never violated it in all his life, no matter how powerful the provocation. It was named after one of the most fearsome denizens of the deserts and plains of the United States: the diamondback rattler.

In short, the rattlesnake code held that, just like the creature that bore its name, no man should attack without having given some notice of his intention. You did not smile at a man and then draw on him, let alone ambush him and fire at his back. The decent man would not set down and break bread with a body and then slay him; nor would he kill an enemy in front of his family. Women and children were altogether sacrosanct, and the man who harmed a woman was the greatest of all cowards and deserving of the strongest disapprobation. To be sure, it was a rough and ready set of rules, but it served to rein in some of the more barbarous practices which might otherwise have taken hold in the country at that time.

In the present instance Denton was trying to figure the extent to which he might be justified in disregarding some of the finer points. By abducting a child of tender years in this way, those who had undertaken the project had, at least to a certain degree, set themselves outside even the unwritten laws by which most men abided.

Still and all, he had never yet fired on a man unawares and it would sit ill with him to start playing such tricks at this time of his life. No, he would give the men their chance, should he catch up with them.

It shed a good deal of light on Jack Denton's character that, though he might agonize over how justified he might be in cutting corners and avoiding certain conventions in taking the lives of the men who had stolen away Marion Fowler's son, he never once asked himself the most important question, which was: should he kill them at all? In his heart Denton had already weighed up the crime and sentenced those who had committed it to death. He wished only to ensure now that he was not later tormented by doubts about not having given them a proper chance to defend themselves before he shot them down like dogs.

Finding Davy Fowler was the simplest job in the world and it would have been an exaggeration to call the business a search in any usual meaning of the word. Denton just walked quietly up into the hills and, before too long, heard the sound of a child's excited laughter. Of all that he had been preparing himself for this was the least expected development. Listening now, it sounded like a little boy romping with a favourite uncle. Mystified in no small degree, Denton made his way onwards, towards the strange sound.

It was easy to see why this area was known as 'the gullies'. The hill up which he was climbing was made of white limestone, which had been split over the course of time into a mazelike network of cracks and fissures, many of them deep enough to conceal a man. Here and there were dotted little caves and hidyholes; it would be an ideal place to hide out. A man sitting quietly in one of the crevices would be quite invisible from the plain below and it would be necessary to search every nook and cranny methodically to find a hidden person.

Unless he was very much mistaken the carefree, boyish laughter was coming from only a dozen yards or so away. Denton stopped walking and listened carefully. In addition to the child's chuckles of delight he could hear a deeper voice, speaking low. Denton drew his pistol and cocked it, before climbing stealthily out of the trench in which he had been walking and scrambling as quietly as he could up and over the edge of formation. At once the voices became clearer and he could see, just six or eight feet from where he crouched, a long, deep gash in the limestone. Without doubt this was the gully that contained the boy and his captors.

'Well,' muttered Denton softly, 'here goes nothin'!' He got to his feet and strolled over to the deep crack in the stone, which he guessed contained his quarry. He was quickly proved right in his estimation of the situation, because he found himself gazing down upon three men and a little boy.

From what he could see the men were playing some game with the boy, just fooling around to amuse him. For his part the child appeared to be having a whale of a time. He certainly didn't seem to be frightened or upset; in fact Denton wondered if he even knew that he had been abducted. Presumably the men had taken him from his aunt's back yard on some pretext or other and he was as happy as a lark.

Denton stood there, just watching the scene for a few seconds, before one of the men spotted him. This fellow let slip an oath and his hand went to his hip, but Denton, with his own gun already out and pointing straight at the man, shook his head. When the other men saw him, they didn't react at all; just kind of froze.

'Davy, you 'member me,' cried Denton. 'I come to eat at your house, you recollect?'

'Yes sir, I know you,' replied the boy, a smile on his face. 'You come up here to play with us?'

'Not exactly, boy. I want you to move away from them two men; you hear what I tell you?'

'Oh, we was having such fun. Do I have to?'

'Yes, you do.'

Showing every sign of great reluctance and with a mutinous and sullen look upon his face, the boy walked away from the men, who watched Denton closely the while. When the child was fully clear of the men, Denton slowly replaced his pistol in its holster, never once taking his eyes off the men who had taken the boy from his aunt's keeping.

When they saw that the man standing on the rocks above them was not about to gun them down in cold blood the tension relaxed slightly.

'I'll warrant you ain't the law,' one of the men said.

'Not hardly,' replied Denton. 'I come to take that child back to his ma, though.'

'Think we're going to let you queer our pitch?' enquired the man who had not yet spoken.

'Reckon as you can stop me?'

It was all the invitation needful to start the fight and ease Jack Denton's conscience. Nobody could say that he hadn't given them their chance. One of the fellows went for his gun and Denton drew and fired twice. Both balls took the man in his chest. The other men had decided that heavier weapons might answer their purpose better, and dived towards the rifle that was leaning against the rock wall of the gully. Denton's third and fourth shots took them both between the shoulder blades.

Under such circumstances, where defiance has been made and the fighting begun, it was considered quite permissible to shoot a man in the back in that way. After all, it was a man's own choice if, after battle had commenced, he chose to show his back to an enemy.

So swiftly had Denton's four shots been fired that the roar of gunfire sounded like one continuous crash, putting the frightened boy who was now cowering in terror in mind of a roll of thunder. It was the sudden, shocking turn of events that had reduced the boy to such a state. The men who had taken him off for what he understood to be a day in the hills at his mother's behest, had been jolly companions who had made every effort to see that the child was not alarmed or made uneasy. They had played games with him and had perhaps really enjoyed the change from their normal mode of life.

At any rate, young Davy Fowler had taken to them and had been having a good time when that hard-faced man who'd been to dinner at his house showed up and shot them down for no reason that the boy could see. He was now terrified of Jack Denton and shrank back in fear as the man jumped down into the gully and tried to persuade him to come along back to his ma.

'Why'd you hurt 'em so?' asked the tearful child. 'They weren't troubling you.'

'Promised your mother I'd fetch you

safe back home,' said Denton. 'I say I'll do a thing, it's what I'll do.'

In a daze the miserable child suffered Denton to take his hand and lead him past the bloody corpses to where the dead men's horses were tethered to a couple of ancient bristlecone pines.

'Can you ride, son?' asked Denton.

'Rode a pony a couple o' times,' answered the boy stoutly. 'I reckon as I can ride this 'un.'

'You don't lack spirit. Let me help you up.'

To his dismay Denton found that the boy twisted away from his very touch, as though he were the carrier of some loathsome disease. A little nettled, he said, more sharply than he intended: 'Those men I killed were villains. You needn't shed tears for them.'

According to Jack Denton's lights he had acted straightforward and honourable and nobody had any cause to reproach him. It irked him to find this child sitting in judgment upon him; the child whom he had saved from the

Lord knew what misfortunes. But there it was. He had long since stopped expecting the world to reward a man for his good deeds or, for that matter, punish him for his wrongs. That was just how things were.

All had gone as smoothly as Denton had hoped and he expected to be back in Jordan's Crossing within the hour, with Marion Fowler's child safely delivered from evil and handed back to her with no fuss or bother. He certainly didn't look to see anybody other than himself and the two sisters any the wiser about what had chanced.

It was an optimistic plan, which had been thrown into confusion when Sheriff Quinn called by Marion Fowler's house not a quarter-hour after Denton had lit out for the gullies. All Quinn was after was a detailed account of what had happened when the three men tried to put the bite on Mrs Fowler. He wanted a written statement for his records and also because he liked to know every-thing that went on in his town. It was in this way that he managed to keep the place so quiet: by stopping any foolishness before it threatened to get out of hand.

Finding the store locked up and Mrs Fowler not responding to any knocking upon the door of her house, the sheriff decided to try at her sister's, who only lived next door. As soon as Margaret Hilton opened the door to him it was as plain as a pikestaff to Quinn that something was amiss; the woman was pale as a ghost and had clearly been crying. After inviting himself in and discovering Marion Fowler in a state of near hysteria, it didn't take long to wrestle the truth out of them.

The sheriff sent Mrs Hilton's maid over to his office to fetch the deputy who was minding the shop; by the time Jack Denton showed up with the abducted child all the machinery had been set in motion to rouse the town and start a posse off in search of the boy.

Truth to tell, it was more than a little

galling to Sheriff Quinn to see that drifter amble into town having rescued the boy before the official law had even, as you might say, got its boots on. Quinn was standing outside the Fowler house, talking to one of his two deputies, when they saw two riders coming on at a leisurely pace. One of the riders was only a child and the other was the man who had been suspected of involvement in the shooting behind the stores on Main Street. Sheriff Quinn's lips pursed in disapproval and he walked forward to intercept the two horses.

But then Marion Fowler came flying from her house, having glimpsed her son through the window. She flew like an arrow from the bow, straight to her son, sweeping him down from the horse upon which he was precariously balanced and crushing him to her breast in a fierce embrace. As she hugged her child, she looked up at Denton, with the tears running down her cheeks, saying over and over again:

'Thank you, oh thank you!'

Quinn went over to the little tableau and indicated to Jack Denton that he was desirous of speaking with him. Denton walked his mount over to one side and the sheriff said softly:

'What happened to those as took the boy?'

'They died,' said Denton succinctly. 'It's a filthy business snatching a child in that way.'

'Happen you're right,' said Sheriff Quinn. 'Anyways, I ain't about to be mourning of them. I'm glad to see Mrs Fowler reunited with her boy.'

The two men said nothing for a spell; both stood watching the affecting sight of the mother rejoicing in the safe return of the child she had all but given up for dead. After a time, Quinn said:

'You fixin' to stay much longer in town?'

'I couldn't say. Why d'you enquire?'

'I'll tell you for why, Denton. You're one o' them types that trouble happens around. I've known a few men like that.

85

I can't precisely blame you for it, but wherever you are, there's apt to be bloodshed. You're like a carrier of some disease. I don't like having men like you in Jordan's Crossing. Without asking you a damned thing more, I can tell by your face that I'm right. You had many peaceful days in your life?'

Denton shrugged and said in a low voice:

'Not over many, no.'

'You're like to be pretty popular after this day's work, so I can't hardly lock you up or run you out of town. But I can tell you, I'll breathe a lot easier when you head off again. You can have your saddle back any time you want, so long as you're heading away from this here town. We understand each other?'

'I reckon,' replied Denton laconically.

5

The sheriff was right about Denton being the hero of the hour as far as the folk of Jordan's Crossing were concerned. The posse that had begun to form when news of the disappearance of Marion Fowler's son came to light was stood down; when they learned that one man had ridden out alone and taken on the gang single-handed they were filled with amazement and admiration. For a few days Jack Denton was the next best thing to the eighth wonder of the world, at least as far as the citizens of Jordan's Crossing were concerned.

One person in the town was not only unimpressed by the rescue but felt a positive distaste and antipathy for Denton and all his works. This was Davy Fowler, who had been the only eyewitness to the cold-blooded way in which the two abductors had been gunned down. It might be argued that the boy was too young fully to appreciate the peril that he had been in and that sometimes bad men have to be dealt with ruthlessly, but it would also be fair to say that the child had seen a side of the quiet-talking stranger that nobody else in the town had yet observed.

Mrs Fowler was mortified by her son's attitude to Jack Denton; the boy would scarcely consent to sit in the same room as the man who had delivered him from the hands of the bandits who had taken him for the Lord knew what purpose. She apologized profusely to Denton on the evening of the rescue, when she invited him to dine with her again. As soon as Davy had swallowed his last mouthful of food he had asked permission to leave the table and had then vanished to his room.

'I'm right sorry that Davy's behaving so, Mr Denton,' Mrs Fowler said. 'I don't think he really understands what you did for him.'

'It's nothin', ma'am, I do assure you. It could be that the shock of the thing has made him a littler nervous round men as he ain't familiar with.'

'You're so understanding. Maybe you're right.'

Since the death of his wife and child at the hands of a band of Border Ruffians, almost ten years earlier, Jack Denton had not looked at a woman in the way that he now saw Marion Fowler. He couldn't say why this might be, nor what this widow had that none of the other ladies he had encountered over the years had lacked, but there it was. He was next door to being head over heels in love, which was a strange and disturbing experience for such a self-sufficient and reserved man such as he.

As for Mrs Fowler herself, she had not yet shown the stranger any more courtesy or interest than that which was rightly due to a man who had come to her aid twice and saved her child's life into the bargain. If she knew or guessed at the strength of Denton's feelings towards her, she certainly gave no external sign of that knowledge.

As is often the case though, when a man is in love, Denton fancied that he detected all manner of hints in her mien, taking her lack of outward signs of affection as being very right and proper and demonstrating the kind of womanly reserve that one would hope to see in a real lady.

After she had poured out coffee for them both Mrs Fowler said hesitantly:

'I said it before, but I must say it again, you been just like an angel to me and mine.'

'Lordy, I ain't in that mould, ma'am. I'm only glad I could be of service.'

'You'll think me right nosy,' said the woman, 'but you've said little about yourself. What do you do? Please forgive me if I'm being inquisitive.'

'Not a bit of it. What do I do? Why, some of this and some of that. The fellow as coined that proverb 'bout being jack of all trades and master of none — why, he might o' had me in mind, and that's the truth. I've rounded cattle, caught bad men, panned for gold, tilled the land. I guess I done pretty well most things since the war. Fiddle-footed, my grandmamma would've called it, God rest her.'

'You don't get lonely? Feel like setting down roots or aught?'

Denton read, or perhaps hoped to read, a deeper meaning into this question and he felt that he ought to explain about why he had no family. He would have hated Marion Fowler to think him no more than some restless saddlebum who couldn't stay in one place. It had been years since he'd spoken of his wife, so the words didn't come easily. Abruptly, he announced:

'I had a wife, you know. Wife and child both. I wouldn't have you think me a man with no use for such things.'

'What happened? Please don't say if you'd sooner not. I don't mean to pry.'

'It was the better part of ten years ago,' said Denton slowly and thoughtfully, 'the year the war began. The official war, that is. Us on the border 'tween Kansas and Missouri, we felt we'd been at war in a small way for some five or ten years 'fore the shelling o' Fort Sumter.'

'I don't know much of that part of the country, I'm afraid. What do you mean?'

'Well ma'am, there was us in Kansas as wasn't too keen on slavery, and we sheltered runaways and such. They called us 'Jayhawkers' and we'd sometimes have some slight friction with those boys from Missouri who were more in favour of the South, as you might say. Sometimes there'd be fistfights and other times shooting. We knew them Missouri boys as the 'Border Ruffians'.'

'Now you say this,' said Mrs Fowler, 'I mind I heard something of the sort. So there was raiding 'cross the border, is that right?'

'That's just so, ma'am. That year, beginning of 'sixty-one, I'd been married two years and me and my wife had a little place on the Kansas side o' the border. She'd give birth to a little girl the year before, and my daughter, Ellie-May as was, she was comin' up to her first birthday when it happened.'

There was a long pause and Denton stared into space, obviously reliving the past. Marion Fowler said nothing, but waited for him to continue in his own good time. After a minute or two, he said:

'I was out in the fields that morning. Heard horses, but didn't think nothin' to it. Then they rode down on me. Whole gang o' border roughnecks, whooping it up. One of 'em fired at me and the ball took me on my head. Only caught me a glancin' blow, but I was knocked senseless. Left me with a scar, you see here?' He tilted his head to one side and pulled back his hair; the woman to whom he was talking could see a long white streak of scar tissue

93

that ran from his right temple and up into the hairline.

'Anyways, when I come to, I smelled smoke. Those bastards — sorry ma'am, it just slipped out — those devils had torched the house. My wife, Theresa, she was lying there dead. They'd used her, then killed her. My baby was asleep in the house, so she was killed too. That's all.'

Marion Fowler's eyes glistened with tears. She had lived a relatively sheltered existence and had never heard anything so horrible in the whole course of her life. Jack Denton stood up.

'I'd best be going,' he said. 'Thanks for your hospitality, Mrs Fowler. You been right nice, listening to me and all. I've told nobody of this before. It's not a thing to be bandied about freely. I'm sure you understand.'

For the next few days Denton kept to himself. He couldn't walk down the street without men and women coming up and wishing to shake his hand, so he took to going off into the hills alone during the day. He didn't know if he had done altogether the right thing by telling his story in that way to Marion Fowler. It had felt right at the time, though, and that was the important thing.

He couldn't get the thought of the woman out of his mind and yet he had no idea how to proceed. He'd never really courted a woman before. Theresa had been his cousin and they had been childhood sweethearts. Marrying each other was just the natural thing to do. This was another thing entirely.

He'd been with whores since his wife's death, visiting cathouses and such, but had never had any emotions about paying for sex. It had been no more than a business transaction, with as little feeling involved as buying a horse or selling a sack of corn.

What he felt for Marion Fowler was nothing like that at all. He wanted to hold and cherish her, look after her and protect her. Denton couldn't recollect having such strange desires before and wondered at times whether he was going out of his mind, or if this was perhaps the first intimation that he was growing old.

★   ★   ★

Three days after the abduction and subsequent rescuing of Davy Fowler, Sheriff Quinn was sitting in his office, examining a sheaf of letters. One of his deputies, Mike Martin, was engaged in brewing up a pot of coffee. It was a little after half past nine on a Wednesday morning. Martin was disposed to be chatty, saying: 'I seed that there Jack Denton this morning, boss. He was up real early. Mooching along, heading out of town. Think we seen the last of him?'

'Without taking his horse?' said Quinn, not looking up from the letter he was scanning. 'I wouldn't have thought so for a moment.'

'What d'you think he's still hanging round for?'

'I couldn't say. Sniffing round the Widow Fowler, I shouldn't be surprised to learn.'

'You think he's fallen for her?'

'What is this, Martin? You thinking to set up as a lonely hearts agency or something? Listen, how much would you be prepared to pay to rent that little log cabin that Mrs Fowler runs as a store?'

The sudden change of topic left Mike Martin, not the brightest of individuals, bemused.

'Why, she giving up the store?' he said. 'I'm surprised to hear it. Why, when her husband died, God rest him, I thought — '

'Shut up and listen,' said Quinn impatiently, 'No, she ain't — from all that I am able to apprehend — giving up the store, nor even thinking of it. I'm asking how much you think the place would be worth to rent, as a businees proposition.'

Having the matter set out in such straightforward and concrete terms made it a lot easier for Martin to consider the question. He might gossip like an old woman on occasion, but Mike Martin was sharp as a lancet where local information was concerned.

'I doubt she makes ten dollars a week from that place,' he replied. 'That's what . . . five hundred a year or thereabouts? She owns the lease for the next few years, so that's all profit. You wouldn't want to make less than five dollars a week or you'd hardly be making enough to eat. So I wouldn't pay more than two hundred a year for the lease.'

It was at times like this that Sheriff Quinn remembered why he had engaged young Martin as a deputy. When you could direct his mind on to a single problem the boy generated the answer like some species of calculating machine.

'Suppose,' said Quinn, 'I told you that six months ago some company up at the county seat had offered to buy the remainder of that lease — there's seven years yet to run — for a thousand dollars? Then upped their offer to twelve hundred when Mrs Fowler told 'em 'no'?'

'I'd say they had a powerful good reason for wantin' that store.'

'Same as I thought. Now we have a bunch of shootings and three men dead. All over that blamed store.'

Deputy Martin thought about this for a space, then asked:

'You think that Denton is mixed up in the business somehow?'

'He is and he isn't. I don't think he knows any more than us what's going on about that store. But he's one o' them fellows as acts as a lightning rod. He attracts trouble like flies to shit. I don't know how they do it, but I met one or two of his brand before. Without doing a damned thing, there's a man who'll stumble into violence and bloodshed. Call him unlucky or what you will, but wherever a man like that goes, he ends up in the midst of disorder and crime.'

'You mean like he's got a hex or jinx or something like that?'

'Couldn't say,' answered Sheriff Quinn. 'It's just how he is. You watch; he'll stay around this town long enough to see the thing out and then he'll dig up and leave. I'm tellin' you, Martin, he's a bird of ill omen and that's a fact.'

★   ★   ★

While the sheriff and his deputy were analysing his character and future prospects in no flattering terms, the object of their discussions was sitting on a rock, shying stones at a nearby tree. Jack Denton was essentially a man of action. Show him an armed enemy or a stranded steer and Denton was your man. He would take smart, prompt action to rectify the situation. His infatuation with Marion Fowler, though, was a horse of another colour and he had not the least notion how to progress further. It was perfectly absurd for a man of his age and experience of the world, but he was acting like a moonstruck calf.

What did men do in such a position? Did they declare their feelings and ask the object of their affections to marry them? Or did they woo the woman gently and slowly, buying flowers and candy and suchlike? Denton had no idea at all how to achieve his goal and this was having the effect of making him a little scratchy and out of sorts. He stood up and wandered disconsolately back into town.

Jordan's Crossing had been founded only twenty years before the War Between the States by a bunch of pioneers who, when they were utterly spent and about ready to drop from hunger, thirst and general exhaustion, had come to a little trickle of water which ran down to a small lake. Finding a reliable source of water in the parched and arid landscape had seemed almost like a miracle of Biblical proportions to the men leading the party; they had decided that setting foot over that stream and camping nigh to the lake was akin to Joshua and his men crossing the Jordan to enter the promised land. So they named the little settlement that sprang up on the spot: Jordan's Crossing.

As had already been intimated to Jack Denton by the town barber, nothing much had happened in the town between that first crossing of the stream and the day when a detachment of Confederate forces occupied Jordan's Crossing, in the final year of the war. It was, as had been confirmed to him by the sheriff himself, a quiet kind of location where nothing much ever happened, which was how the folk in the little town liked things.

When Denton got back to town there didn't seem to be any more reason to be there in Main Street than there had been for staying where he'd been. He felt thoroughly dissatisfied and half-minded to pull out the next day. It was the thought of Marion Fowler that held him back from such a rash move. He wanted, above all else, to visit the store and speak to the lady herself, but was hindered by the terrible fear that he was making a fool of himself.

In the end he did nothing, which was not uncommonly the case when Denton couldn't come to a definite decision. He moped around town for the rest of the day and then took early to his bed.

In consequence of having gone to bed so early the previous night Denton awoke next day at the crack of dawn. To be exact, his eyes were open and he was lying restless before the first glimmering of the sun had touched the distant hills to the east of Jordan's Crossing. He tossed and turned for a while, then decided that he might as well be up and about as lying there doing nothing and quite unable to sleep.

He accordingly rose and dressed,

then slipped quietly down the stairs and out through the door. There was nobody about at that hour and Denton wondered what time it actually was. It could hardly have been later than four or five in the morning. He walked along the street idly, in the general direction of the livery stable.

On the corner where stood the Royal Flush the owner had erected a tall metal rod, bearing a pasteboard sign extolling the virtues of the saloon. From time to time, Sheriff Quinn grew vexed at the sight of this metal pole blocking the free passage of pedestrians and ordered its removal, but just at the moment the sheriff had other and more important fish to fry and so he tolerated its presence.

What was curious this day was that there appeared to be something oddly different about the arrangement. As he drew near Denton saw what it was. Somebody had placed a large, irregularly shaped lump of material on top of the post, which was about six feet high.

Whatever it was had seemingly dripped some liquid down over the poster. Even in the near darkness it was plain that something was not right.

Denton went closer to see what was what and then recoiled in horror when he realized what the state of affairs was. In the middle of the night, while everybody was sleeping, somebody had crept up to the Royal Flush and jammed a decapitated head on to the metal spike that held up the pasteboard advertisement. Drops and half-congealed clots of blood had dripped down from this ghastly object, besmearing the poster with gore.

Jack Denton had led a livelier life than most and taken part in some pretty grim goings-on, but never in all his life had he seen anything like this. Worst of all was where this was the head of a woman. The long hair which dangled down two feet below the ragged stump of the head, was matted with dried blood. All in all, this had to rank as the most terrible sight that

Denton had ever seen in his whole life.

A lamp was burning in the livery stable, so Denton sprinted over to see if anybody was about. The owner was pottering around in the barn and he was most surprised to be disturbed at that ungodly hour.

'Why, it's Mr Denton, isn't it? You're an early riser sir, I do declare! How may I help you?'

'I need to speak to the sheriff. It's right urgent.'

'I doubt he'll thank you for raising him at this hour. I'd leave it for a little, were I you.'

'It can't really wait. I think he'll want to hear of this now.'

'Well, you don't say! Go back down the street apace, 'til you come to the saloon. Turn left, just 'fore you reach it and Sheriff Quinn lives right at the end of that little road. You can't miss it for he has a shingle in front of his house, announcing who he is.'

'I'm greatly obliged to you.'

You would have to go a long way to

find a man less squeamish than Jack Denton but, all the same, he was anything but enthusiastic about passing the post near the saloon that bore such a grisly burden. He averted his gaze as he reached the Royal Flush and hurried down the narrow lane that turned off to the left. Just as the fellow at the livery stable had said, there was the house with the shingle hanging in the front yard, informing the world that Nathaniel Quinn lived there and that he was the sheriff of Jordan's Crossing. It wasn't often that Quinn permitted himself any vanity, but he was proud of his position in the town.

As Denton had guessed would be the case, even before the man running the livery stable had told him, Quinn was not best pleased to be woken before dawn. When he saw just who it was who had been raising Cain on his front door, he was even less pleased. He threw open a casement on the first floor and yelled down:

'What the hell's so important that it

can't wait until dawn? Oh, I might have guessed. It's you, Denton.'

'Sheriff, I wouldn't o' disturbed you without cause. You best come and see this right now.'

'See what? Wait, don't tell me. Let me guess. Somebody's dead, am I right?'

'Why yes, but I can't think how you knew.'

'It's you, Denton. You always seem to be associated with dead men. This somebody you killed?'

'No, it ain't,' said Denton indignantly. 'And if you don't want to know 'bout this, I'll leave it for others to let you know.' He turned to walk away, seriously annoyed.

'Don't take on so. I didn't mean nothing by it. Stay there and I'll be down directly.'

6

Two days before Jack Denton arrived in Jordan's Crossing a group of men were sitting around a campfire about five miles from the town. The evening air was mild and the twelve men were relaxing after a satisfying meal. All but two of them were smoking and they looked as cheerful as could be. They also, by the by, looked like what they were: a bunch of bandits and ne'er-do-wells.

Sitting on a rocky outcrop, somewhat higher than the other men, was an elegant and dandified little man with a swarthy face and a neat pencil moustache. This individual was picking his teeth delicately. The men scattered around the clearing below him were a mixed bag of various nationalities and ages. Two looked Mexican, one was a half-breed and several looked as though they might be Negro. All had one thing in common, though, which was that they looked like men one would not wish to cross without having an excellent reason for doing so.

Many — perhaps most — men at that time carried weapons of some sort with them a lot of the time, but these fellows were armed to the teeth. One man had two pistols tucked in his belt, another had a pistol in a holster and an enormous Bowie knife in a scabbard at his other hip. Around the little clearing in the pinewood heavier weapons were scattered in casual profusion: rifles, army carbines, scatterguns and even an old flintlock musket.

The buzz of conversation which filled the circle of light around the fire died down as the little man on the rock stood up and made it clear that he was about to address them. When there was complete silence, he said:

'Gentlemen, I want to tell you a story. It is not a fairy tale from long ago, such as you tell to children, but something that chanced in this very area not ten years since. You all recall the war? Some of you fought in it, like me.'

There were one or two raised eybrows at this statement and a few of the men exchanged meaningful glances, the import of which was not lost upon the man standing above them.

'What,' he said with a look of comical dismay upon his handsome face, 'you do not believe me? You didn't know that I, Carlos Mendez, was an officer in the Yankee army? Nevertheless it is true. I, your captain, was a captain indeed. There now, what do you say to that?'

If anybody other than Mendez had rambled on so self-indulgently the men lounging around there would have shouted at him to get on with it and perhaps made mock of him. Nobody even dreamed of taking such a liberty with Mendez, who had in the past given ample evidence of both his savagery and also his capacity for taking offence.

'Anyway,' continued Mendez, 'that is

by the by, as they say. Near to the end of the war a troop of greycoats came along the road here and took over the town of Jordan's Crossing. They made everybody get out. Was that not a remarkable thing to do?

'After two or three days they left. There were perhaps sixty of them. Cavalry, carts, two field guns and various other things. After they left the town a tragedy befell them. The Yankees descended upon the rebels and demanded their surrender.

'It was almost the end of the war, but those men still had spirit. Did they surrender? No. They drew themselves into battle order and issued defiance.'

Some of the men were now growing distinctly restless as they listened to Mendez's story. They suspected, quite correctly, that he could have compressed the tale into a few dozen words, but that was not the little man's way. He had a theatrical bent and a flair for play-acting and drama to which he gave full rein on occasions such as this.

'Then what happens? I will tell you. The Federal soldiers, they had artillery too. They shelled those poor Rebels and then, when it came to hand-to-hand fighting, they killed them all. Even the prisoners they took. You are shocked? It is what they call in France *fortune de guerre*.

'Did I say all were killed? I forgot to say that one man did escape. He did this by pretending to be dead and then, later on, after the bloodlust of the Yankees was spent, he revealed himself and they took him prisoner and did not kill him.

'Mind you, my friends, later on he wished that they had killed him. You know where he went? Rock Island camp in Illinois. Ah, but that was a terrible place for a man to be. The prisoners there, they died like flies of the typhoid, starvation and I don't know what all else.'

Since they had begun to follow Mendez, his band of cut-throats growing over the course of the months until there were now a dozen of them, every one of the men there that evening had benefited greatly from his leadership. The little Spaniard had the brains and ferocity which made him a born leader of men. That he had once held a commission in the Union Army was news to them, but it fitted in well enough with what they had seen of his ability to control a group of wild and unpredictable thieves and rogues. At any rate, they knew that Mendez would only be spinning them this tale now to show them a way of making even more money and so they sat quietly, like a class full of children being told the story of *Mother Goose*.

'This rebel, he knew that unless he got out of that camp at Rock Island he would starve to death or die of the bloody flux or who knows what other dreadful thing. He had to buy his way out and, luckily for him, he had a secret to sell.

'I say luckily, but it was not so lucky for him in the end, because who do you think he came to with this great secret? Yes, it was none other than Captain Mendez, who just happened to be stationed at that prisoner of war camp.

'And now, my friends, you want to know what this great secret was that this man had been keeping to himself. A secret that he thought would buy his freedom from that hell-hole. I tell you the truth now, what this man told me is worth twelve thousand dollars to every one of you men sitting there.'

The figure that Mendez gave them was beyond all imagining. They often had a a few hundred dollars each as their share after some robbery, and some of them had had as much as $500 or $600, but $12,000! If it had been anybody other than Mendez promising such fabulous sums they would have dismissed it as the ravings of a madman. But they knew the man. Here was somebody who always spoke straight and would have scorned to pledge more than he could deliver. If the man up on that rock said that there was $12,000 to be had by every one of them, then that was almost certainly the literal and unadorned truth.

'You wonder what this fellow said?' continued Mendez, 'That he thought he could bribe me, a captain in the Federal army, to forget my duty? Here is where you learn what we are doing here, right now. He said that this unit he had been with had been retreating from . . . well I don't recall the name of the town or the battle there. It does not matter. But they had salvaged from the collapsing Confederacy a large part of its gold reserves. They had, on a wagon, four hundredweight of gold bullion.'

There was a stirring around the camp; men sucked in their breath noisily while others muttered, 'Shit!' in awestruck tones. Mendez surely had their attention now and not one of those men any longer evinced any sign of impatience. They were mesmerized by the thought of so much treasure.

'Those rebels knew that the Yankees were hot on their tail and did not want to see the gold fall into the hands of those same thieving soldiers who had caused so much havoc in the South. What did they do? They buried it. They threw everybody out of that little town, so nobody knew what was going on and then they found an empty lot: one that was being used as the town's dump. It was covered in old lumber, broken furniture, useless pots and pans, all manner of trash. They carefully removed it all and then dug a big hole. Into this they placed the two chests, each holding two hundredweight of gold. Then they filled in the holes, put the rubbish back in the empty lot — and there you are!'

Somebody called out: 'Just how much is this gold worth?'

'Figure for yourself,' replied Mendez. 'There are two chests, each containing two hundred pounds. That is four hundredweight in total. Allowing now sixteen ounces to the pound, gives us six thousand, four hundred ounces of the precious metal. At current prices, that makes a hundred and sixty thousand dollars.'

'What are we waiting for?' growled one of the men, 'Why are we sat here and not riding into Jordan's Crossing this minute?'

Another man had a sudden, dreadful thought.

'Hey,' he called out, 'what's to've stopped that fellow as told you of this having told others since, or gone to dig up this gold for his own self?'

'These are intelligent questions,' said Mendez approvingly, 'and they are tied together. As to that miserable, starving scarecrow of a greycoat being held captive at Rock Island having told another of this secret: alas, he died not five minutes after having revealed the details to me.

'Why do we not ride down on to that town and just take the treasure? There are two good reasons. First is where there is a sheriff there and many men who might oppose us. They might not let us start digging in their town

118

without asking what we're about.'

Mendez stopped for a moment and lit a cheroot after fumbling around in his jacket for a lucifer. He took his time lighting and drawing on the thin cigarillo, until somebody asked:

'What's the other reason? I reckon as we could hold our own 'gainst a bunch o' store clerks and such.'

'It may be so,' admitted the Spaniard. 'It may be so. But there is another complication, an unlooked-for difficulty. The empty lot where that Confederate gold was hidden is empty no longer. There is a store on it now, with a solid and substantial floor. Before we can even start digging for that gold we must first take over the store and dismantle the floor.'

There was dead silence upon hearing this unexpected conclusion to the tale. On the face of it seemed that the men were stymied, but every one of them had sufficient faith in their leader to know that he would hardly have brought them this far unless he had a plan for dealing with these setbacks. And every single one of those men was feeling almost sick with lust for his $12,000.

Mendez had played his hand with consummate skill, dangling the gold before them so that they felt it was almost within their grasp, before snatching it away again by telling them of the obstacles which stood between them and their $12,000 apiece.

Mendez said nothing further, but smoked quietly as the men digested this unexpected information. He did not think that it would be precisely delicate or politic to reveal to them his efforts to gain access to that store by legal means: methods that would not have required him to put together this band of brigands. Had that cursed, foolish woman accepted his fine offer of $1,200 to surrender the lease on her miserable log cabin, Mendez would by now have taken possession of the place and ripped up the floorboards to get at all that bullion.

But no, she was stubborn, that one. He felt instinctively that he could have offered not $1,200, but $12,000 and she would not have budged. There was doubtless some sentimental attachment to the store, which blinded the woman to her own best interests. Well, that's how it was sometimes in this world.

'You set us a pretty riddle,' observed one of the men slouched around the fire, 'but I know you, you already worked out the answer too. Why 'n't you let us have it, hey?'

'Did you never learn at your mother's knee,' responded Mendez, 'that patience is the cardinal virtue?'

'Can't say as I did,' said the man who had spoken. 'You goin' to lecture us on theology or tell us how we're going to get that there gold as you tell of?'

'It's no great mystery. I want three of you to ride into town tomorrow. Find a place to stay and look around a little. Then, the next day, I want those men to offer the woman running that store, of which I shall provide the details, fifteen hundred dollars to surrender the lease. If she does so, then we need only close down the store and set up a mine inside it. A gold mine.'

'Supposin' she won't play?' said another man. 'What'll we do then?'

'Ah, you run ahead of yourself, my friend,' replied Mendez. 'Let's try the quiet way first and then, if that won't answer, we can think of stronger measures.'

One man, who had not yet spoken, said:

'I don't get it. Why'd those men bury this gold? They must o' known the war was over; why didn't they just divide it up and share it out among themselves?'

'Why, they were honourable men!' exclaimed Mendez mockingly. 'The gold belonged not to them but to the Confederacy. They hoped that their sacred cause would rise again and that their defeat was only a temporary setback.

'You know what Sir Christopher Wren found carved on a stone when he looked around the burned-out ruins of the old St Paul's Cathedral in London, after the Great Fire? It was the single word in Latin: *Resurgam*. I will rise again. Ah, you look blank, perhaps you did not have the classical education?'

'Never had any sort o' education to speak of,' said the man, 'classical nor otherwise.'

'Well then, those Confederates believed that the gold would pay for their people to rise again against the Yankees. That's why they didn't steal it for themselves.'

★ ★ ★

The following day three of the men set out for Jordan's Crossing. Their instructions were simple: they were to offer Mrs Marion Fowler up to $1,500 to give up the lease that she held on the general store. If she might yield more readily to some threats, then they could try those as well. If nothing was to answer, the three of them were to return to the camp that Mendez and his followers had established, where they would all take counsel together and see what might be done.

Of course, no more was heard of the three men. Snatching the little boy after the offer of money had been declined had been purely their own idea and not something that Mendez would have wished to happen in a thousand years. Not because he was sentimental about children, but rather because such an action drew needless attention to the little store and might cause sharp minds to wonder what was so special about the place that such lengths would be resorted to to gain control of it.

After they had waited patiently for three days and nights without hearing anything from the men who had gone to Jordan's Crossing, Mendez dispatched a lone rider to visit the Royal Flush to find out what the gossip of the town was and see whether it would shed any light upon the disappearance of their three comrades. It didn't take this scout long to hear about the shooting at night and the subsequent abduction of the young boy. He also learned of the stranger who had single-handedly rescued the child and killed those who had taken him prisoner.

'He sounds an interesting one, he does,' was Mendez's comment when the news was relayed to him. 'I hope I meet him before we are done. He is perhaps a worthy adversary.'

'This ain't nothing to the purpose,' said one of the band. 'What's to do now?'

Mendez said nothing for a short while. He was not altogether happy with the turn of events. All else apart, he preferred the rapier to the blunt instrument. It had been his hope that they would have been able to acquire the store without violence, then just remove the floor, recover the gold buried beneath it and drive it away in a wagon. Now it looked as though there would be bloodshed, violence and chaos. It would be messy. But there, though; it could not be helped.

'I will tell you what we do now,' he said. 'We prepare to take the gold by main force.'

'Thought you said as that wasn't a smart idea,' objected somebody, 'on account of there being a sheriff and various men who might oppose us by force of arms.'

'Have patience. That is so. Which means that we needs must remove the sheriff and the stronger men. Make sure that they are not in town when we arrive there for our treasure.'

'You're a good leader, Mendez,' remarked a man, 'but you surely are a wordy bastard. What have you in mind? Just tell us straight, without a lot of flowery talk.' Mendez eyed the fellow with some disfavour, but made no comment.

Then he announced brightly: 'But of course, you are right. I told you we stand to reap twelve thousand dollars each. We will have to refigure. Two of you can have fifteen thousand and the rest of us must have our shares reduced accordingly. Who volunteers for this extra money?'

These men were all of them a little too long in the tooth even to think about buying a cat in a sack of this sort. They waited to hear what would be needed to earn an extra $3,000. When Mendez realized that there would be no mad rush for an increased share, he said gaily:

'Ah, you all wonder what task could be worth fifteen thousand dollars, is it not so? I will tell you. Before riding into that little town we need to make sure that the sheriff and his deputies are not at home. We also should see to it that most of the younger and more active men are away from town too. Otherwise we'll be getting into a shooting match and I don't think any of us would care for that.'

'Longer you take to tell us what's what, the more suspicious we's a-growin',' remarked somebody; this observation elicited a chorus of guffaws and cheers. Mendez scowled.

'You want it plain? Very well. Two men must kill a family known well in town. A family whose deaths will provoke the men of Jordan's Crossing to fury. Then, those men must lead a trail away from the town, so that a posse goes after them, but does not catch them. While this is happening, we will ride into the town for long enough to seize the gold and make off.'

'You mean, send that sheriff and his boys off on a snipe hunt and hope that half the men in town go with them?'

'You have the case in a nutshell,' said Mendez, 'but whoever takes on this job must know that they will be hanged out of hand if the posse catches up with them.'

'How we goin' to make sure that the sheriff knows about these murders?'

'I thought,' replied Mendez casually, 'that whoever kills this man and his family might cut off one of the heads and take it to town. Just to let them know what to do next, you understand.'

One of the older men called out: 'I'll do it, Mendez. I ain't much of a one for being squeamish. Long as this ain't some scheme to cheat us or make cat's-paws of the man as does this thing.'

'I'm in as well,' said another of the men. 'I could surely do with fifteen thousand dollars.'

7

Sheriff Quinn was a tough customer, but he found that the sight of a woman's head jammed casually atop a sign advertising the attractions to be found at the Royal Flush, made his gorge rise. Unwilling to let Jack Denton see this weakness in him, Quinn turned away from the hideous spectacle and found the owner of the bar-room standing near by, gazing in horror at the sight. The sun was now peeping above the horizon and the scarlet blood was rendered vivid in the early morning light.

'Mother of God!' exclaimed the saloon keeper. 'What in the name of all that's holy is this?'

Knowing that it was likely to take a while to track down the real culprits, Sheriff Quinn released some of the anger and disgust he was feeling by directing it against the man who had placed the sign on the public highway.

'Haven't I told you a hundred times not to obstruct the way with your damned notices?' he thundered. 'You never get the message, do you? I'm telling you now: from this day forward if I see another of your placards anywhere other than on your own property you'll be spending the night in my cells. You got that?'

'Sure, Sheriff,' replied the man meekly. 'Just as you say.'

Other early risers began to gather: men who were getting ready to open the shutters on storefronts or ride out to the fields around the town. They all of them gazed in utter astonishment at the decapitated head 'That's Lizzie Booker,' one said in a low voice, 'Jim Booker's wife, you know.'

'I recognized her,' said Quinn. 'Anybody been up to their place lately?'

It appeared that nobody had, nor did anybody know how the couple had been getting along recently. It was the sheriff's experience that murders of a wife could almost invariably be laid at the door of the dead woman's husband and he had no reason to suppose this case to be any different. The other immediate suspect in any murder was the person who apparently found the corpse and first reported the matter to the authorities. Quinn had no love at all for Jack Denton, but he certainly didn't have him pegged for a woman killer.

'I'll need a statement from you later,' he said to Denton. 'Call by my office and either me or one of my deputies'll take it.'

'What do you make of this here?' asked Denton. 'I seen a heap o' bad things in my time, but never the equal of this.'

'I'll be riding out to the Booker place later, see what account her husband gives of himself.'

Denton gave a short laugh.

'This weren't no domestic crime,' he said. 'Why would her husband come and leave the head here?'

Although he had decided not to discuss the business with the young man Quinn couldn't help asking, his voice heavily laden with sarcasm:

'Maybe you'd like to tell me how you read it, if you're so sure of who didn't kill her?'

'If it wasn't her husband done it, then you'd think he'd fight tooth and nail to protect his wife. I reckon as you'll find he's been killed too.'

'Oh you do, do you? Anything else?'

'They have any children?'

'Two. Boy and a girl, aged about seven or eight.'

'Well then, they're dead too.'

Sheriff Quinn stared long and hard at Denton, half-wishing he could persuade himself that he was looking at a suspect in the case. It was infuriating because, much as he disliked Denton, he could see at once the sense in what the fellow was saying.

'Just be sure to come by the office later, all right?' he said at last.

The sheriff left Lizzie Booker's head

up on the spike for a good two hours before giving one of his deputies orders to remove it and stow it somewhere secure. He was beginning to think that Denton was right: that Jim Booker had most likely not been responsible for this terrible crime. If that were to prove the case, then he would need to recruit a posse to hunt down whoever had been involved in the deed. Allowing the citizens of Jordan's Crossing to see the woman's head would fill them with anger and pity, making them more apt to volunteer to ride with him to track down the killer.

It was a cold-blooded decision, but Nathaniel Quinn had not maintained the peace in that town for so many years without having to aid him a certain cold and ruthless streak. He wanted above all else to bring to justice whoever had killed Lizzie Booker and he would use any tactics at all that tended towards such an end.

It was gone nine before Quinn, accompanied by Mike Martin, set off towards the Bookers' farm, which lay four miles or so to the south of town. The Bookers were fairly prosperous and spent freely in Jordan's Crossing. Jim Booker was a pleasant man, if a hard bargainer, and most people in town recognized him and his wife and children by sight. As they rode from town Martin said:

'D'you think we'll find Booker was answerable for this, boss?'

'I couldn't say. I've an idea not.'

'I don't get why a man would chop off his wife's head and then travel four miles to advertise the murder in the middle of town.'

'What do you make of that Denton fellow?' asked the sheriff. 'You formed any conclusion about him?'

'Seems all right. It was him as found the head, weren't it? You suspect him?'

'Of killing Lizzie Booker? No, not a bit of it. I just wondered what you made of him, is all.'

'He ain't a man I'd care to get crosswise to.'

'No, I reckon not.'

The two of them reined in when they came within sight of the stone-built farmhouse where the Bookers lived. There was no curl of smoke from the chimney, nor any other sign of life about the place. Quinn reached out the carbine that he carried in a scabbard at the side of the saddle and cocked it. Taking his cue from the sheriff, Mike Martin drew his pistol and they walked their horses on to the farm. When they reached the yard, Sheriff Quinn called out loudly:

'Hallo! Anybody at home?' A dog barked, but there was no other response to his hailing.

Without taking his eyes off the house Sheriff Quinn dismounted and looked towards the blank windows, wondering if he were being watched by an enemy. What if the man who had so savagely mutilated Lizzie Booker were taking a bead on him at that very second? He scrutinized the windows closely and saw that, although it was now broad daylight, the drapes had not been drawn.

'You want I should go round the back and set a watch there?' Mike Martin asked. 'Make sure nobody escapes that way?'

'No, I don't think that's needful. Lend me a hand and we'll see if the door has to be stove in.'

As it turned out the stout and imposing front door of the Booker house was unlocked and unbolted; the sheriff and his deputy could just walk straight in. As soon as they set foot in the house both men were immediately aware of the coppery stink of fresh blood. A lot of blood, judging by the smell. Martin went into the front parlour and pulled back the drapes. Then he cried out like a frightened girl at the sight that he beheld.

As the light flooded into the room the deputy saw that he had unknow-ingly paddled through a veritable lake of blood. Four corpses lay on the carpeted floor, one of which lacked a head. Gauging by the sheer quantity of blood, Martin guessed that the others had had their throats cut. For a moment he felt giddy and faint, but then he recollected that his boss was near by and would have some pretty scathing things to say if his deputy showed signs of fainting or having a fit of the vapours. Gritting his teeth and turning his eyes from the horror, he called out:

'Sheriff, you best come in here.'

That anybody could murder a whole, entire family in such a frightful way was beyond the comprehension of either Quinn or Martin, especially where two of the victims were children of tender years.

As they returned to town Quinn wondered idly how the thing had been achieved. There was no sign that Jim Booker had fought or even struggled. Had more than one person been involved in the killings? Not that it really mattered. Sheriff Quinn had sworn a private oath to himself that when he managed to track down the men who had carried out this atrocious massacre there would be no pussy-footing about with arrests and trials and suchlike. He would have them hanged out of hand, just as soon as he had caught them.

Denton knew in his bones that the murder of the woman, part of whose remains he had stumbled across early that morning, was all of a piece with the trouble over Mrs Fowler's store. He couldn't rightly say how he knew this to be so; simply that it was without doubt the case.

Sometimes, when he was riding the range, Denton had a sudden premonition that rain was coming. From time to time, the feeling was stronger than that and he knew that thunder and lightning would be accompanying the rain when it came. He'd never really asked himself how such a sense worked; he only knew that it had never yet played him false. It was the same now. 'Storm's coming!' Denton muttered to himself, 'Storm's coming and looks like I'm the only as knows it.'

Had it not been for his interest in Marion Fowler this was the point at which Jack Denton might, in the usual way of things, have been thinking of moving on. After all, he owed nothing to that town or the people in it. He'd tried to warn that stubborn sheriff, but it seemed like nobody wanted to listen to him. Well, so be it.

But he knew, even as he thought this, that he was whistling in the wind. There wasn't the remotest chance of his digging up and leaving. Even if she didn't have the same feelings for him that Denton had for her he knew that he couldn't just leave her fate to chance. He would at least be obliged to protect Mrs Fowler from the oncoming storm.

★ ★ ★

By some miracle Marion Fowler had not yet heard the news that was

140

sweeping through town like a brushfire. She had got up, breakfasted and come straight to the store. There had been no customers so far that morning to inform her of what was the talk of Jordan's Crossing. When Jack Denton walked through the door Mrs Fowler's face lit up with a pleasant smile, which warmed his heart and gave him cause to hope that his affection might be returned, if not right now then at some later date.

'Why, Mr Denton, this is a surprise. What brings you here?'

It was a plain fact that Denton had never studied the art of approaching an important subject in a roundabout or circuitous manner.

'You got any folks you could go and stay with?' he asked. 'Out of town, I mean?'

'I don't understand. Why should I go and stay away from here?'

Feeling that there might not be much time for fancy talk, Denton asked another question:

'You know a woman called Lizzie Booker?'

'Yes, I know Lizzie. She brings her children here most weeks. Why do you ask?'

'She's dead,' announced Denton bluntly. 'Somebody killed her and then took off her head.'

'Took off her head? Whatever can you mean?'

'I mean just exactly what I say, Mrs Fowler. She's dead and after she was dead, leastways I surely hope it was afterwards, somebody chopped her head from her body and then brought it to town. Stuck it on a post nigh to the saloon.'

Marion Fowler looked at the softly spoken man standing near the counter and shivered, as though somebody had walked over her grave.

'You're serious, I guess?'

'You think I'd invent such a tale to scare a lady?' asked Denton. 'Not hardly.'

'Why should I leave town, though, because of it?'

142

It was a question that left Denton stumped for an answer. He knew, deep inside, that some very violent men would be coming to the town directly and that, for reasons at which he could only guess, they would be making a beeline for this very spot. How he knew this he was quite unable to say, let alone explain to another person. He said simply:

'Mrs Fowler, do you trust me?'

'I'd trust you with my life, Mr Denton. After what you did for me in bringing back my boy I wonder you ask the question.'

He digested this for a bit, then observed: 'You've not answered my question. Do you have anybody you could go and stay with?'

She shook her head. 'There's nobody,' she replied. 'All my kin are dead. There's only me and Davy.'

Jack Denton said nothing; he appeared to be lost in thought. Then he said: 'If you trust me, then may I hope that you'll take any advice I offer, as tends to you and your boy's safety?'

'Yes, you can be sure of that. Tell me what to do and I'll do it.'

There was a fair-sized crowd of men gathered in front of Sheriff Quinn's office. Just as he had calculated, the sight of a woman's head stuck up on a post had roused every man who saw it to a high pitch of anger, mingled with a burning desire to wreak vengeance upon those capable of such beastliness. It would hardly be necessary to badger men to ride out after those who had killed Mrs Booker, and this was before word had spread about the fact that the dead woman's husband and children had also been butchered, having their throats cut like hogs.

Denton eased his way through the crowd and entered the sheriff's office. Mike Martin, seated at a table and surveying a ledger, barely glanced up to say:

'I'll take your name directly. Just wait outside with the rest.'

Quinn, who had been rummaging

144

around in a closet, turned at that moment and saw Jack Denton standing before him.

'You're a bird of ill omen, Denton, and no mistake,' he said. 'What brings you here?'

'Wondered if you wanted me to ride with your posse, is all. I know I ain't from this town but I can shoot straighter than most and I ain't afeared o' much in shoe leather.'

'No,' said Sheriff Quinn, 'I make no doubt as that's true, leastways as far as it goes. But I'll decline your offer of help.'

Although he was secretly relieved that Quinn did not want him to be a member of the posse that was forming up, Jack Denton was at the same time a little irritated to be thought unworthy of such a position.

'Mind tellin' me why you don't want me?' he asked.

'It'll be my pleasure. You're a Jonah, Mr Denton. You bring ill fortune wherever you set your foot. I believe I

145

told you before, I've known more than one man of the same brand. You can't help it, I'll allow that ready enough, but that don't mean I want to ride side by side with you. I don't. Men die when you're near 'em, ain't that the fact?'

'Just as you wish,' replied Denton. 'Recollect, though, that I offered.'

The worst judgements made upon us by others, and the ones that sting the most, are those that contain more than a grain of truth in them. So it was in this instance. Denton was honest enough to admit to himself that there was a good deal in what Sheriff Quinn had said and that he had not in the past brought a deal of luck to his partners.

Still, he had wished to stay in town to keep an eye on Mrs Fowler and her interests, so he should be grateful really to Quinn for declining his offer of service so swiftly and definitely. He just wished that he could feel that the sheriff realized the full extent of the danger.

Jack Denton did the sheriff an injustice in thinking that that individual was incapable of adding two and two together and obtaining a reliable sum of the two digits. He knew very well that the murder of Lizzie Booker must surely have some connection with both the shooting behind Marion Fowler's store and the adbduction of her son. It was against all reason that the quiet little town of Jordan's Crossing should so suddenly be afflicted with bloodshed and violence from a number of independent and unrelated causes. It was a sporting certainty that in some way that he had as yet been unable to fathom the murder of the Booker family was all of a piece with the snatching of Marion Fowler's son, and that both crimes were associated for some obscure reason with that store she ran.

Even Nathaniel Quinn's best friends would perhaps have hesitated to describe him as a marvellously intellectual man. He was, on the other hand, nobody's fool and he could, given time enough, see his way through a brick wall, as the saying goes. In the present situation, his knowing that the men who had slaughtered the Booker family were connected in some way with those others who had taken Davy Fowler gave him an edge. He knew that a large group of men were probably mixed up in the business and that he would accordingly need the biggest posse he could recruit in order to take them on.

The only thing that he didn't know was that that group of men had been split in two and that he was being deliberately led on a decoy hunt, simply to draw him away from the town he looked after.

In the end, almost bankrupting the town council's budget for the coming year in the process, Sheriff Quinn engaged fifty-two men to ride after the killers of the Booker family. There had been no sight like it since the end of the war and everybody in town watched as the troop of men rode off to track down and execute justice upon the murderers. Stores were closed and fields would be left untended for a few days, until they found the men.

Each member of the posse carried enough vittles with him for two days, so it was likely that for that length of time at least, all the most lively, vigorous and young men in Jordan's Crossing would be away from their homes. That this would have the effect of leaving the town unguarded and defenceless did not occur to anybody, other than Jack Denton.

Along with the rest of the town Denton watched the posse ride out; then, when they had gone, he turned his steps to a store that offered to provide tinware, agricultural implements and firearms, all at moderate prices.

Bill Trenton, the owner of the store, was a frail and ancient individual, whose infirmities rendered him unable even to mount a horse these days, let alone ride one. He had accordingly remained behind to tend his store.

When Denton entered the store old Mr Trenton's face lit up with pleasure. Like everybody else in Jordan's Crossing, he knew the story of how this young man had tackled single-handed the gang that had taken Mrs Fowler's child, had killed the kidnappers and rescued the boy, bringing him safely back to his mother.

'Good day to you there, Mr Denton,' said Trenton. 'How may I serve you?'

'You sell guns, I think?'

'Yes sir, that we do. What might you be after?'

'You have rifles?'

'Surely do. You want that I should fetch a few out?'

'Yes please, but in a minute. What about scatter-guns?'

'Got them as well. What is it you're after, rifle or shotgun?'

Denton rubbed his chin meditatively. 'Well,' he said. 'I want one of each. What about powder? You sell that, I guess?'

'Depends on the quantity. How

much you after?'

'Could you let me have five or ten pounds of the stuff?'

'Five or ten pounds? Mr Denton, pardon me for askin' and feel free to tell me to mind my own affairs and so on, but looks to me like you're getting ready to launch your own personal war.'

The man who stood in front of him did not appear to be in the least degree discomposed by the suggestion.

'You said you'd bring me out some rifles to show me, I think?' he replied mildly.

8

Pete Owen and Dave Jaeger, the two men who had volunteered to commit a shocking murder and then draw the sheriff and his posse away from Jordan's Crossing, ranked as two of the most cold-hearted and wicked men who ever walked the earth. Jaeger had worked for a time in a slaughterhouse and had a fund of amusing anecdotes about the suffering he had inflicted upon the animals before he finally killed them. Pete Owen had been a white slaver, tricking girls into going south, across the border into the brothels of Mexico, on the wholly fictitious promise of well-paid careers on the stage. The two of them were cut from the same piece of cloth and Mendez could not have hoped to find better men for his purpose.

After they had left camp Owen said

to his companion: 'You think Mendez is right about this family? That their death'll rouse the whole town?'

'He's a deep one,' replied Dave Jaeger. 'He seems to know what's what. If he says so, then I'd guess it's true. Hey though, we can have some fun here, I'm tellin' you!'

'I was thinking the selfsame thing my own self. We'll have to kill the man first, but I want some fun with the woman. With the risk we're like to run, I reckon we're deservin' a little something extra.'

Neither man needed to spell out what they meant by this, each of them being the type of person to commit rape as soon as another man would drink a cup of coffee. Not only were they supremely callous and uncaring, they were neither of them overburdened with brains.

Had they been just a little brighter one or the other of them might perhaps have stopped to consider that they would be lucky to escape with their lives from this little adventure. The thought of the $15,000 had mesmerized them and now the thought of being able to carry out a rape during a murder spree had driven from their heads thoughts of any possible hazard to themselves.

That night Jaeger and Owen burst into the Bookers' home and butchered four people. They killed Lizzie Booker last of all, after having had their way with her. After she too was murdered, Owen decided to lie with her again; but this was too much for Dave Jaeger to stomach.

Later, after Owen had sliced off the dead woman's head, he chaffed his comrade about his lack of enterprise.

'Hell,' he said, 'that ain't the first time I done it with a dead person. You want to try new experiences, man. You're like an old woman sometimes.'

Jaeger alone rode into Jordan's Crossing with Lizzie Booker's head and affixed it to the poster outside the saloon. He was very nearly detected in the act by Jack Denton, who came along just as Jaeger was making his way down the gap between two buildings with a view to leaving the town. When he got back to the Booker house, Jaeger was raring to leave at once, in order to lay their trail for the posse, but Pete Owen swore that he wouldn't leave until he had a good breakfast inside him. So the two men fried up some eggs and brewed some coffee.

Leading the sheriff and his men off on a snipe hunt was an exceedingly delicate undertaking. On the one hand, it would be no good making such a clean getaway that there was no trail to follow, causing the posse to give up and return home after half a day. On the other hand, those laying the trail obviously did not wish to run the risk of being caught and hanged.

Jaeger and Owen actually left the Booker house an hour or so before Sheriff Quinn and his deputy arrived. Neither of the lawmen got round to entering the kitchen, so horrific was the scene that had greeted them in the front parlour. Had they done so they might have discovered that the stove was still warm from the breakfast that the killers had made there.

★ ★ ★

Denton left the store with a hunting rifle, a scatter-gun, a box of caps, a length of rope, some fuse and a five-pound keg of fine-grained gunpowder. It was lucky that he had been carrying a fair sum of money on him. He didn't think that he'd be the loser by his transactions, whatever chanced in the next twenty-four hours. He could do with a rifle, and at a pinch he could always sell the shotgun if it proved surplus to his requirements. No doubt the powder would come in useful at some time as well, and having a coil of rope in the saddlebag was no bad idea.

After equipping himself with the various things that he felt that he might need if, as he was sure would be the case, there was a confrontation with men interested for some reason in Mrs Fowler's store, Denton went back to the hotel room he was staying in and made one or two preparations.

The clerk at the hotel was able to lend him a hacksaw and, when he was alone in the room, Denton used this to shorten the barrel of the scattergun until he had turned it into a stubby little weapon. He fashioned a sling from a length of rope and then used this to hang the sawn-off weapon over his back. He stripped down his pistol and made sure that the cylinder was rolling smoothly and that the mechanism was operating perfectly. Then he filled his flask with powder, loaded the rifle and went back out on to Main Street, ready for anything.

As they rode with the fifty-odd men towards the Bookers' farm Mike Martin turned to his boss.

'You think we need this many men?' he asked. 'I never seed a posse like it before in my life.'

'Does no harm to be prepared,'

replied Sheriff Quinn casually. 'You never know what might happen.'

'Come on, sir, level with me. Why'd we need so many bodies?'

Quinn thought for a moment, then decided that he might be well advised to take his deputy into his confidence.

'What it is, Martin,' he said, 'is that I'm half-persuaded that there's a gang at the back of this murder. I don't think it was some random, wandering maniac.'

'So why'd they put poor Mrs Booker's head up on a pole?'

'I don't know and that's the God's honest truth, but I aim to find out. And when we run those boys to earth, howsoever many there might be, I want to make certain sure that we've more on our side. There, that make it clearer?'

It did, and Deputy Mike Martin was pleased and proud that for once his boss had deigned to share his thoughts with him. Quinn was a notorious one for playing his cards close to his chest and this was the most open he'd been for a long time. Martin felt emboldened to venture an opinion of his own:

'I was thinkin', you know, it's a strange sort o' circumstance that we been as quiet as quiet can be in town for years now and then, all of a sudden-like, we get three lots of killing in as many days. You reckon that's a coincidence? I don't.'

Sheriff Quinn turned his head and fixed his deputy with a cold eye.

'You been thinking, hey? Don't let me catch you doing such a thing again. Happen as I can do enough thinking for the two of us.' Then, seeing Mike Martin's crestfallen expression, he relented.

'Don't fret,' he said. 'I'm only joshing. I swear, sometimes I think you might have the makings of a sheriff in you. Your mind works in the right direction, at any rate.' But he would not be drawn further on the possibility of any connection between the present enterprise and the other violent and illegal events of the past few days. After a time his deputy subsided into silence again.

★ ★ ★

Carlos Mendez had never planned to be a bandit leader. He was in fact a minor member of a noble Spanish family that had settled in Mexico at the beginning of the century. One or two indiscretions in his youth, though, had caused him to have to leave Mexico hurriedly. His family had bribed the right people and he had ended up at West Point. The army had not suited him and, if the war had not come, he would without doubt have resigned his commission and sought his fortune elsewhere. Not that being an officer in the US army had been unprofitable; far from it.

The greatest error of his life had occurred after he had learned the whereabouts of the fabulous haul of gold bullion lying buried beneath an empty lot in a little town. He had a hankering to see his family once more and had crossed over the border just as the war was raging in Mexico between the supporters of the Emperor Maximilian and those who favoured the native Mexican politician, Benito Juarez. It was inevitable that his own relatives should support Maximilian, under whom they had flourished and become even more wealthy.

After foolishly throwing his lot in with the regime, Mendez found himself sentenced to death following Juarez's triumph. At the last moment, even as he was being led out to face the firing squad, the sentence had been commuted to a life of hard labour in a penal colony. After three long years Mendez's escape was contrived and he fled to the United States, where he gathered around himself a band of outlaws. A born leader of men, he had fashioned them into something like a military unit, all the time bearing in mind those four hundredweights of gold that lay buried in the little town.

Owen and Jaeger had been instructed to draw the sheriff and his posse far enough away from town for them to be obliged to spend the night out in the open. Once dusk came Mendez and the others would descend upon Jordan's Crossing and dig up the gold. There would be no need for any violence in the town; indeed, it was Mendez's fervent hope that there would be no unpleasantness at all.

The last thing he wanted was for the posse to return to town and then start out again at once, this time hunting for the men with the gold. As he saw it, there would be no trouble at all and certainly nobody would be hurt in the town. He and his men would move very quickly to enter the store, rip up the floorboards and then dig in the earth beneath. True, they might make a mess of the store, but there would be no murder done and no cause for anybody to chase after them.

This last was an important point,

because they would need to carry away all the gold in a cart and that would necessarily slow them down and make a swift getaway all but impossible. If Owen and Jaeger did as planned and caused the posse to spend a night away from town, Mendez and the others would have a twelve-hour start at least, so there would be a good length of time during which to escape.

While he was waiting for word from the lookout posted above Jordan's Crossing that a posse had left the town Mendez stood a little apart from his men, smoking and thinking. While he was doing so one of the others came up to him.

'You believe that those two will escape hanging?'

The man who asked this question was Tom Barnaby, like Mendez, himself a former soldier in the Union Army.

'Sure, why not?' Mendez replied blandly. 'They are cunning and resourceful men, are they not? I have every hope that they will rejoin us, as we planned, tomorrow night.'

'You ain't thinking, perhaps, that with those two out of the way and their thirty thousand shared between the rest of us, that'd be another three thousand all round?'

The two of them were speaking very quietly, so that they were not apt to be overheard.

'This is a very strange notion, friend Barnaby,' Mendez said. 'Do you mean anything by it?'

'Only that we might increase our own shares even more, if any mischance were to befall a few others.'

There was silence and the words lay between them. Without either assenting to or dismissing what the other man had said, Mendez murmured thought-fully:

'You are a deep thinker, it seems. We will talk further on this, perhaps.' Then, to signal that the conversation was at an end, he walked back and joined the rest of the men, who were lounging around the clearing, smoking and idling their time away by playing poker for twigs and stones.

★   ★   ★

When Jack Denton appeared again in the store Marion Fowler was taken aback at the change in both his appearance and his manner. Gone was the diffident and quiet man whom she had rather taken to; in his place was a sharp-faced and brusque character who was carrying a rifle in his hand.

'Time to shut up shop,' he announced with no preamble. 'You must return to your sister's home and stay indoors there. Don't go to your own house at all and don't, as you value your life and that of your boy, set foot outside your sister's house until I give you leave.'

These instructions were issued in an almost peremptory fashion, as though from an officer to a private soldier who was expected to obey without question. Marion Fowler was a little irritated to be bossed about in this way by a man who was, despite all that he had done for her, virtually a stranger.

'May I ask why?'

'I'd sooner not have said, but as you make a point of it, there'll be men coming here soon to this place. They find you here, they'll most likely kill you. They know where you live, on account of you had those letters from the company up at the county seat. You want to survive this, you do as I bid.'

'You don't mince your words.'

'There's no time for fancy talking. You trust me, like you said you did, then just lock up this place, let me have the key and go straight back to your child. And don't show yourself out and about. All else apart, I'd hate for you to get caught in the crossfire.'

The woman looked at him, startled.

'Crossfire? You expect gunplay?'

'Ain't a betting man, but I'd wager a hundred dollars on it,' Denton replied shortly.

Even for two men as cold-blooded and unimaginative as Pete Owen and Dave Jaeger, laying the trail was becoming a little nerve-racking; they were slowing their mounts to a sedate walk from time to time so as to leave very clear prints in a patch of mud, and occasionally they stopped entirely to light little fires so that the smouldering embers would be there as a signal to the following posse, indicating the way in which they were travelling. Each of them was beginning to wonder to himself whether they hadn't taken a wrong turn in pursuit of that extra $3,000. Fat lot of good $15,000 would do either of them if they ended up dangling at the end of a rope.

The result of these misgivings was that Owen and Jaeger said less and less as the day drew on. They were both wondering whether the time wasn't approaching that they should simply bolt for it and be damned to the money.

'What say we ride on at a canter for a

space?' suggested Jaeger eventually. 'I reckon we been going at a walk long enough.'

'You may have a point.'

It was now about five o'clock and there was still a good deal of daylight left. By their calculations the posse should have set off round about midday and it was a certainty that they would have proceeded first to the farmhouse and picked up the trail from there. Owen and Jaeger had left many clear indications of their route around the Booker place and had then tried to make it a little harder, so that those following them might need to dismount and examine signs carefully. What they couldn't have known, though Carlos Mendez had guessed it would probably be the case, was the strength of the posse. Quinn's posse was no half-dozen men trotting along for their five dollars a day payment, but a body of fifty-two men for whom the money was of secondary consideration.

The two men they were tracking had

been given over to beastliness and base conduct for so long now that they had lost sight of how abominable some of their actions would seem to decent men. Of course they knew that killing a woman and her children was a hanging matter and were also aware that removing a woman's head after killing her was a terrible crime in the eyes of any right-thinking person.

The truth was, though, that they didn't really feel the same way as other folk and so they hadn't gauged that there would be quite so many men from the town on their trail.

The sheer size of the posse bearing down upon them was ultimately to be the undoing of Pete Owen and Dave Jaeger. Because there were fifty-two men it was possible to divide up in to smaller forces and send out scouting parties; the sort of tactic that would have been impossible had there only been a dozen men.

At about one that afternoon the man who had been watching Jordan's Crossing on behalf of Mendez and his gang came riding back to their camp with the news that a very large body of riders had set out from the town.

'I never see such a posse,' he said, 'not in all my born days. Pete and Dave'll have their work cut out, I'm telling you.'

'How many would you say?' asked Mendez. 'More than thirty?'

'Hell, I shouldn't wonder if there weren't twice that number.'

'Good, good.'

Mendez clapped his hands to attract the attention of everybody scattered around the glen. When there was silence he spoke.

'We must make ready to move. By the grace of God, fifty of the toughest and most energetic of the town's men will be sleeping away from their homes this night. We will, I think, be able to arrive there and simply take over the store.

'As long as we do not behave badly I don't look for any opposition. I don't want any shooting or killing. Nothing is to take place that would provoke anybody into pursuing us when once we have left. I hope that I make myself plain.'

'What about Pete Owen and Dave Jaeger?' called somebody. 'We're picking up with them later, right?'

'Of course, of course,' lied Mendez smoothly. 'They have performed for us a most valuable service. Surely they have earned their money. But now let us prepare to break camp and ride down to the town. And recollect, there is to be no blood shed in the enterprise. Not one single drop.'

★ ★ ★

Those who saw Denton that afternoon knew that something was afoot, although they couldn't have said what. He made no attempt to conceal from anybody the fact that he was now

171

armed to the teeth and, with the posse riding out, it was not hard to see that some trouble was now expected by Jack Denton in the town itself. Men greeted him and he responded affably enough, but did not say what it was he feared or why he was carrying three firearms now. One man spoke outright.

'You plannin' on fighting a war, Denton?' he asked.

'Some fellow from long ago,' replied Denton, 'one o' them ancient Romans maybe, he said: 'If you want peace, then prepare for war'. I reckon that's sound advice. That's what I'm doing. By which I mean, I hope for peace, but I'm making ready for the other thing as well.'

★   ★   ★

Most posses are too small to be able to consider putting out flankers, but with fifty-two men to play with, that is just what Sheriff Quinn did. He set four men to ride out at a furious gallop, ahead of the main body of men, two on either side. These men were to ride in a wide, sweeping direction, as fast as they were able, to scout ahead.

Quinn had a strong suspicion that there were more than one or two people mixed up in this business and that the massacre of the Booker family had been part of a bigger game. He was of course quite right about this, but he had not realized that the main force of those he was up against was now behind him and making its way to Jordan's Crossing.

Before sunset one of the pairs of riders whom the sheriff had sent on ahead had spotted their quarry. These men had ridden hard and fast up into some low hills. From there they had a bird's-eye view of the rough terrain below them and were able to discern a thin plume of dust, which marked the track of the men they were pursuing. After taking counsel together one of them headed back to inform Quinn, while his companion continued to ride along the crests of the hills, keeping a watchful eye upon the men suspected of the murders.

When Sheriff Quinn knew for certain-sure that he and his boys were on the right track and that, from what could be seen, the two men they were hunting were alone and not part of a greater force, he led twenty of his men forward at a smarter pace than they had previously been adopting.

Without the need to be constantly halting and examining various signs and indications and now with the sure knowledge that the men they sought were directly ahead of them, the sheriff and his chosen men could make quicker time. As they drew closer to their prey the flankers waved from the high ground on either side, to show that they could see the men ahead of Quinn.

So it was that Pete Owen and Dave Jaeger found themselves in the very position that they had hoped at all costs to avoid: with twenty determined and angry men bearing down on them from behind and three other men ahead of them riding down from the hills to hold the road against them.

When there is any possibility at all of escape, men will fight to the death in their attempts to break free of the coils. When, as in this case, the situation was quite hopeless and they were outnumbered eleven to one, a shoot-out would have been no more than an elaborate form of suicide. While the hope of life is there few people will choose to squander it. Owen and Jaeger, on seeing that escape was impossible and that they were outgunned to a great degree, decided to parley and perhaps talk their way out of trouble. That they should even believe for a moment that such a course of action might be possible was a clear indication of the limited nature of their mental abilities.

9

The riddle of the attraction that Mrs Fowler's store apparently held for various people was finally solved by Jack Denton when he stood alone in the middle of the place, with nothing to distract him. He had asked to be allowed to look after the key for that very reason, so that once he knew that Marion Fowler was safe and sound he could focus his attention on her store and examine it thoroughly at his leisure. So it was that, at about the same time that Sheriff Quinn and his posse caught up with Pete Owen and Dave Jaeger, Denton had completed a meticulous search of the store and was standing in the middle of it, just thinking hard.

Having established that neither the business itself nor the location of the building were anything special, all that was really left was the possibility of something valuable being concealed about the premises. After going over the place methodically Denton had decided against this as an explanation for two reasons. The first was that there was simply nowhere to hide anything. The walls were not hollow and there was no roof space. Looking upwards allowed one to see the underside of the roof: there was no ceiling. Nor was there a crawlspace under the building, there being barely three or four inches between the floorboards and the dirt below.

The second reason for Jack Denton's doubting that anything of value was stashed somewhere in the building was that if that was all there was to it there would have been no need to offer a large sum to acquire the lease of the building. Putting himself in the position of somebody who knew that some treasure was hidden in the fabric of a little building such as this, Denton knew that he would not set out to attract attention to the matter by offering to rent the place. Surely, the easiest option would be simply to break in quietly, with no prior warning, and remove whatever it was that he wanted?

If whatever these people were seeking could only be obtained by taking charge of the building for a spell, then the solution was simple: the valuable item or items must be buried beneath the building.

Once he had figured out the matter a broad grin split Denton's face. Despite the dangers of the situation, with which he would most likely have to deal that very day, he could not help but feel enchanted that he had worked things out. Presumably those whom he had interrupted when they were breaking in on that fateful evening had been working out the practicalities of ripping up the floorboards and digging beneath the floor.

⋆   ⋆   ⋆

Pete Owen was not a sensitive or imaginative soul, so he did not grasp so readily as his friend that they were likely to be choking to death at the ends of ropes in a matter of minutes unless they made terms with the men who had captured them. When it was obvious that they were surrounded there had been a brief moment when they might have tried to shoot their way out of trouble; this had passed when both men saw how overwhelming were the odds against them.

Having thrown down their weapons and put up their hands Owen and Jaeger were left in a poor position for bargaining. Nevertheless Dave Jaeger thought it worth a try. He spoke to the grim-faced men surrounding him and his partner.

'You'll be wanting to know what this is all about, I guess. Here's the way of it. Take us back to town now and I'll give you chapter and verse on the whole matter.'

It was a last desperate throw of the

dice, but if Jaeger really believed that it would be enough to save his life, that only went to show how remote was his and his companion's grasp of the ordinary rules of society. There was not one man in that posse who would have set free those men, even if offered $1,000 in cash. So vile had been the crime for which they had been apprehended that no man in his right sense could have expected to live for long after capture by the friends and neighbours of the dead family. Despite all this, Sheriff Quinn thought it worth questioning the man.

'Well, speak up man,' he said. 'Your life is hanging by a thread. What caused you and your friend here to undertake such a business?'

Incredible to relate, Dave Jaeger actually felt that he discerned here a ray of hope and his heart lifted. He and Pete Owen were sitting on their horses, weaponless but unharmed. Flight was impossible because they were so hemmed in and surrounded by the hostile men who made up the posse. Nevertheless Jaeger thought that he might yet save his own skin even if it meant sacrificing that of Owen.

'You promise you'll not harm us without a proper trial?' asked Jaeger, showing a degree of optimism that bordered on imbecility.

'I make no promises,' replied the sheriff. 'I tell you, though, that I'll listen to all you say and take it into account. Come, time's wearing away. Let's have it.'

The thought of losing that $15,000, which a short while ago had been so tantalizingly close, was a torment, but even Jaeger realized that there could be worse things befall a man than the loss of money.

'We was to draw you away from town,' he replied. 'There's a bunch of men due to ride down on your town tonight. There's a fortune in gold buried 'neath one o' the stores. Ride hard, and you'll like as not catch 'em in the act.'

'Marion Fowler's store, that'd be?' asked Quinn.

'Yes, that's the one. None of this was our idea, see. There's a greaser called Mendez as come up with the idea.'

'You got aught else to say on this?' enquired Sheriff Quinn in an amiable enough tone. 'If so, don't hold back, you know. Your life might depend upon it.'

Relief was flooding through Dave Jaeger and he was congratulating himself on having played a poor hand with masterly skill.

'No, I reckon as that's all,' he said quite chirpily, as though addressing an equal. 'You know as much as I do now.'

'Good, good,' said Quinn, still affable and reassuring. Then he turned to Mike Martin.

'Hang the pair of them,' he said.

So well did he imagine that he had been getting on with the sheriff that for a moment Jaeger didn't grasp the full import of Sheriff Quinn's words. His mouth opened and closed like that of a stranded fish; eventually he said:

'I told you all I knew.'

'That you did, boy, and I'm right grateful. You didn't really think it was enough to buy your life though, surely?'

Both Dave Jaeger and Pete Owen died hard, kicking and choking for several minutes after they were suspended. The men of the posse watched the deaths impassively, feeling that those responsible for such atrocious murders thoroughly deserved to suffer so.

After the executions were over Sheriff Quinn raised his voice and addressed the men.

'If what that rascal said was true,' he said, 'we've got bad men entering town any time now. We'd best ride like the wind and see how soon we can be back.'

'It'll take us a good two hours or more to get back to Jordan's Crossing, even at a gallop,' called somebody.

'I know it,' said Quinn, 'and there's nought to be done about it.'

★   ★   ★

While the posse from Jordan's Crossing was executing summary justice upon the two men who had massacred the Booker family, Carlos Mendez and his band had halted on the edge of Jordan's Crossing and were making their final arrangements. The intention was simply to break into Marion Fowler's store, rip up the floorboards and begin digging right in the very centre of the place, that being the spot at which, according to Mendez's informant, the bullion was buried. With a team of ten men all exerting themselves to the utmost, it surely could not take more than an hour or so to unearth the treasure. The whole enterprise would be completed before anybody in the town had managed to get round to organizing any opposition to their actions.

Sheriff Quinn and his deputies being out of the way, together with forty or fifty of the youngest and toughest men of the town, Mendez and his boys had every reason to suppose that they would not be hindered in their activities by anybody. They could hardly have been expected to know that, even as they sat there on their horses chatting about the moves that they would make as soon as they entered town, they were all under observation by a capable and determined individual who was exceedingly ill-disposed towards them.

Jack Denton watched from the roof of Mrs Fowler's store as the little group of riders, accompanied by a horse and wagon, pressed forward and began moving down Main Street in his direction. He slithered down the shingled roof to the eaves, then lowered himself into the same back alleyway where he had shot a man dead a few days earlier. There were more men than he had expected, but not so many that Denton was in any way daunted by the prospect of facing them.

It might perhaps be wondered what possible motive Jack Denton could have for thwarting the endeavours of a bunch of ruthless bandits intent on mounting an assault upon a little town upon which he had never set eyes until a few days previously. The answer was simple. If there was something of great value hidden beneath Marion Fowler's store, then either she would be entitled to part of the value of whatever it was or, at the very least, a reward of some kind for the recovery of the thing.

It had not escaped Denton's notice that the widow was finding it something of a struggle to make ends meet on what she was able to make from running the store; anything extra would surely be welcome. He had in any case more than half decided to stay in town and court the woman for whom he had now formed a powerful attachment. Helping her to a claim in a fortune would do him no harm in that department at all.

The sight of a troop of horsemen such as those who were riding with Mendez was not a common one in

Jordan's Crossing. As the riders trotted down Main Street more than one person stared uneasily, wondering what these rough and dangerous-looking men were after.

They rode past the saloon and the hotel without halting, so they were presumably not seeking liquor or beds for the night. Those on Main Street at that time of day, as evening was approaching, stopped what they were doing and frankly watched the party of men, to see what they were going to do. They soon found out. The riders stopped outside the little general store run by the Widow Fowler and then dismounted.

Three men in their riper years stood across the street and watched in amazement as two of the strangers took down metal crowbars from the wagon that they had brought with them and proceeded to break open the door of Mrs Fowler's store. They made no effort at all to conceal what they were about; the screech of metal on metal, followed by the crack of splintering wood echoed across the street.

'Lord a mercy!' exclaimed one of the oldsters. 'Sheriff ain't back yet, I s'pose?'

'Not he,' replied another of the old men. 'Doubt he'll be back afore the morning.'

'Reckon as we should brace those boys our own selves?' suggested the third of the men, who had not yet spoken. 'This is our town, when all's said and done.'

The other two men shook their heads slowly.

'We get ourselves killed,' one of them opined, 'those boys'll still do as they wish. Can't see the profit in it.'

Having agreed to do nothing the three men carried on standing and staring, thinking that, if foiling the strangers' intentions were not possible, a detailed description of the men and an account of their doings would be the next best thing to offer Sheriff Quinn when he returned to town.

Having broken open the door to the store, the raiders fetched lamps and spades from the wagon and carried them inside. They were unhurried in their movements, although they did not aim to waste any time. To everybody's relief, it looked as though the folk of Jordan's Crossing were content to adopt a policy of 'Wait and see'.

It seemed wise, even so, to post a sentry outside the store while the rest of them set to and ripped out the floorboards, preparatory to digging in the dead centre of the earth below the floor. But, as long as those two mad fools Owen and Jaeger had done their part, the sheriff and his deputies, along with most of the able-bodied men in town, would be miles away now with no possibility of their immediate return.

Jean Baptiste, a fiery little Creole who had served in a Zouave regiment during the late war, was detailed to guard the entrance to the store and make sure that nobody came in or interfered with what was being done.

The Frenchman was a swaggering little bully and was hoping to have the chance to tell somebody to mind his damned business and get the hell out of there. His opportunity came sooner than he had expected.

As he stood there, picking his teeth and awaiting his chance to frighten some innocent person off by snarling ferociously, Baptiste observed a timid-looking young man making his way along the boardwalk towards him. Being the kind of man that he was, Baptiste judged how dangerous a man was by the extent to which he bragged of his prowess, or the number of fights in which he engaged, or by various other kinds of behaviour. By his standards the fellow approaching him now was probably a right soft one.

The noise from inside the store was considerable, with the loud creaking of floorboards being ripped up and snapped asunder and the shouting of men as they argued with each other as to the best method of accomplishing their purpose. Because of the din Baptiste did not at first catch what the man who was now facing him at a distance of six feet or so had said.

The man had taken his stand and had spoken so quietly that his words had been swallowed up in the racket emanating from the store. Now that Baptiste looked harder at the fellow it struck him that he had perhaps been mistaken at first about his character. He looked a little more formidable now that he could be seen close up. Baptiste spoke to the man:

'What you say? I can't hardly hear you.'

'I said, you want to fight?'

For a moment, Jean Baptiste was not sure that he had heard aright. In his experience challenges from one man to another were delivered with many expressions of bravado and outward displays of courage and defiance. This quietly spoken man might have been offering to buy him a drink.

He gazed stupidly at the man, who

went on, in that same soft tone: 'You going to fight, or you want me to step closer and spit in your face? Or maybe you're just yellow?'

On hearing that fatal word 'yellow', as deadly an insult as any man had ever used against him, Baptiste was gripped by a murderous rage.

Instinctively he reached down to the pistol at his belt, but the man who had provoked him had been ready; at the first twitch of Jean Baptiste's hand the other man drew and fired twice. Both bullets took the little Frenchman in the chest and he dropped lifeless, tumbling off the boardwalk and into the dusty road. The man who had shot him sprinted back the way he had come and then dodged into the gap between two buildings to retrieve the rifle that he had left there. As soon as it was in his hands he cocked it, then leaned round the corner and aimed towards the store.

The shots that killed Jean Baptiste were heard clearly above the noise of the digging in the store. The men paused in their work and one went to the window to see what was what.

'Baptiste's had it,' he announced.

'Carry on, you fools,' said Carlos Mendez. 'One of you stay by the window to keep watch. Don't show yourself though.'

It had been understood by all that there was to be no bloodshed in the town if humanly possible. The last thing any of them wanted was to find the large posse that had lately gone haring after Owen and Jaeger taking it into their heads to pursue them as well. Killing anybody from the town would be a certain-sure means of guaranteeing such a thing.

Denton waited patiently, with his rifle trained on the entrance to the store. Since he had started shooting, the men in the building must know that they were under assault. Under such circumstances the rattlesnake code was clear: once shooting had begun it was every man for himself and all involved were assumed to be on their guard.

Thirty seconds after he had killed Baptiste two things happened to Jack Denton. The first was that he realized that the men in the store were not about to be lured out into open battle by the death of one of their number. The second was that a man about thirty yards behind him, discharged an ancient fowling piece in his direction.

One of the three old men who had observed the goings on concerning the Widow Fowler's store had not been satisfied with the notion of leaving the matter to the duly appointed law. He had gone home to fetch the scattergun that he used to hunt game with which to supplement his meagre diet. It was hanging ready loaded upon his wall, so he just lifted it down and went by a circuitous route back to the store.

His way took him along the alley running at back of the store; as he approached the place from the rear he noticed, to his right, a man whom he took to be one of the gang, standing there bold as brass and aiming a rifle.

The figure was silhouetted against the light, or Jed Scott would have recognized him as the young fellow who had rescued Davy Fowler.

Old Jed was used to positioning himself in a good spot and then taking careful aim at his target. Firing like this, however, on the spur of the moment and while in an excited state of mind, quite spoiled his aim and the shot went high. Luckily for all concerned the weapon he was using was a single-barrelled shotgun. After firing, Jed went loping off down the alley again.

The range was short enough for the boom of the shotgun and its effects to sound pretty much simultaneously, at least as far as Jack Denton was concerned. A shower of wooden splinters fell over his head and shoulders as he heard the shot and, at the same time, felt a stinging pain in his right shoulder. It was not a solid thud such as a bullet would have made and he guessed immediately that it indicated nothing worse than his catching a few pellets of buckshot. He whirled round, but there was no sign of the man who had fired at him.

This time when they heard a shot the men digging beneath the floor of the store did not stop, only hesitating for a fraction of a second before redoubling their efforts. All had the same thought: that getting four hundredweight of gold bullion out of the town might prove a harder row to hoe than they had anticipated.

In keeping with his scrupulous code of honour Denton had intended, if at all possible, to confront the men who were robbing the store and fight them man to man. Since they were not minded to do so and would rather send a sneaking assassin to shoot him in the back, he would have to resort to his other scheme: more certain but a little too cowardly for his taste.

One could hardly blame Denton for assuming that the man who had shot at him from behind was one of the bandits, nor would anybody think any the less of him, really, for adopting the safer course of action for foiling the theft of whatever it was that lay under Marion Fowler's store.

After buying the keg of powder and other supplies, Denton had rigged up a primitive but deadly petard or mine. He now brought out his box of copper percussion caps. These little things fitted over the nipples on the cylinder of his pistol and were also used on percussion-lock muskets. Each cap was smeared with a generous dollop of fulminate of mercury; an entire box of caps would contain perhaps two ounces in total of this most sensitive of explosives. The slightest tap was enough to detonate it.

Denton secured the box of caps over the bung-hole of his five-pound keg of fine-grained powder. When he'd first rigged up the thing he'd had it in mind to mine the road leading from town.

Now another idea occurred to him.

10

It looked as though the men who were occupying the store were not planning on coming out on to the street to fight. The question Denton was now asking himself was whether they would shoot at anybody passing down the street? He received his answer when a man rode into Jordan's Crossing and trotted his horse right past the store without being gunned down.

This was enough for Denton. Leaving his rifle propped up again in the narrow space between the two buildings, he picked up his mine and began walking in a diagonal line, which would take him across the street and past the wagon standing outside the store.

He had already observed that this was an old prairie schooner, though now lacking its canvas hood. On the side facing the street hung a pick and shovel; if this cart conformed to convention Denton expected to find a large wooden pail hanging on the other side. He hoped that this would be the case, else he would be left feeling mighty foolish. To his relief, as he approached the other side of the wagon he saw that there was indeed a bucket hanging there.

From the corner of his eye Denton observed a man watching from the window of the store, so he sauntered on, as though he were just an ordinary man crossing the street. He did not wish to attract undue attention to himself or to run the risk of being blown to atoms. Placing the keg of powder in the pail could be the more discreetly undertaken because of the pail's being on the side that was concealed from the lookout at the window. Somehow, without breaking his stride, Denton managed to deposit the keg in the bucket, keeping the box of caps facing upward.

Jack Denton continued to walk to the

opposite side of the street, half-expecting the while for somebody to shoot him in the back. As he crossed the road old Mr Scott was scuttling back home, having terrified himself out of his wits by actually firing at somebody. His eagerness to tackle the suspicious gang had evaporated quite away and he was now content to leave it to others to deal with the men in Mrs Fowler's store.

Having gained the boardwalk on the other side of Main Street Denton strolled into the barber's shop; in there he found a bunch of men who were watching the unfolding drama as though it were a musical theatre or some other kind of harmless entertainment. He was greeted affably enough, those present having seen him gun down Jean Baptiste and thus having concluded that he was working in opposition to the men who were now holed up in the Widow Fowler's store.

'You been hit, Denton,' one of them remarked.

Those few stray pellets of buckshot that had struck his shoulder had been enough to draw blood, it seemed. His shirt was all over crimson down the right sleeve.

'It don't signify,' Denton said. 'Is there a way out the back here?'

'Surely is,' the barber answered. 'What you fixin' to do?'

'You all keep away from that window,' said Denton, ''less'n you want to get showered in broken glass.'

It was obvious to the men in the barber shop that Denton was not spouting idle words and they hastily moved back from the window at front of the shop.

Having been let out at the back of the shop into an alleyway similar to that running behind the stores on the opposite side of the street, Denton sprinted along until he figured he could cross back over the road without being seen by the man standing by the window of Marion Fowler's store. Then he made his way back to retrieve his rifle.

The two iron-bound chests had been buried only four or five feet below the surface; by now both of them had been hauled out of the shallow pit which had been re-excavated. The chests were far smaller than most of the men had anticipated. When you think of a hundredweight sack, it is generally full of some commodity such as flour or rice, which take up a good deal of room. Gold is considerably heavier than most other substances, though, and it was wondrous to consider that each of those small boxes really contained two hundredweight of the precious metal.

There were stout locks on the chests, which the men were at first eager to break open with crowbars, until Mendez said irritably:

'Have you men lost your senses? There'll be time enough for that later. Just load them on to the wagon, so we can be clear of this place.' His men did as they were bid.

Meanwhile, Jack Denton was calculating the best point at which to lay his ambush. The first question to decide was an easy one: which way would the wagon be travelling out of town? Since the road passed through town, leading in one direction to the Booker place, the bandits would naturally be making their escape in the opposite direction. They would, after all, hardly wish to run the risk of bumping into the posse, which had set off towards the Bookers' farm earlier that day.

Having picked up his rifle, Denton ran as fast as he was able towards the outskirts of town. He was aware of being watched from practically every window he passed. The folk of Jordan's Crossing appeared to have decided, by common consent, that staying indoors until the present crisis had been resolved was the wisest policy. This suited Denton well enough, for it meant that he would be able to carry out his plan without worrying about civilians getting caught in the crossfire.

Just after the last building on the very edge of the town there was a low stone wall, which ran for a hundred feet around a disused field. This wall looked as though it would be ideal for Denton's purposes. He felt that time was now pressing and that whatever it was that those fellows were digging up might at any moment be found and taken away on their wagon.

There were two extremes to be avoided. On the one hand he did not, of course, wish to be so close to the wagon when his petard was fired that he was himself injured or even killed in the resulting explosion. On the other hand he had to be close enough to be sure of hitting a pretty small moving target with one shot.

In the end he took up his position some thirty yards from the roadway and crouched, resting his musket on the wall for stability.

There was still no sound of hoof-beats, so Denton figured that he probably had a little time in hand. He was able to work out roughly where his target would be when once the wagon hove into sight, and he aligned his weapon accordingly.

While he waited Jack Denton turned over in his mind the plans he had for the future, all of which included Marion Fowler as a participant. He had come to think of this precious thing, whatever it was, that had been dug up from beneath Mrs Fowler's store as his gift to her, almost like a bridal dowry. He was, he hoped, no more mercenary than the next man, but surely, once he had settled all accounts with the men who had threatened her wellbeing, and had secured for her some large sum of cash into the bargain, the woman for whom he had fallen would be inclined to view him as a favoured suitor.

As his mind turned pleasantly towards thoughts of future matrimony, Denton heard the creaking of wagon wheels, combined with the drumming of horses' hoofs. It was almost time for the final act in this affair.

There was nobody about on foot; the town's folk were still evidently feeling it safer to remain in their homes and business premises until these men had left Jordan's Crossing. This made Denton's task all the easier. He sighted down the barrel as the wagon came into view. It would have to be a superb shot and he would only have one chance at it. If he missed the least he could expect was for a veritable hail of gunfire to be unleashed in his direction.

He tracked the wagon, but its bouncing and jolting made the chances of getting a clean shot all but impossible. Then one of the wheels hit an obstruction of some kind, causing the driver to rein in the horses and check that the axle hadn't been damaged. For a second or two at least the wagon was stationary.

Most of the riders were bunched together near to the wagon, and for a moment Denton's view was obscured by one of the horses as it moved forward. He prayed that the rider would

206

not choose to halt in front of the pail, but by great good fortune he moved on.

Denton thought that he was unlikely to have another such opportunity; he drew in a breath, held it and then, with infinite care, squeezed the trigger. The .5 ball flew at 1,400 feet per second towards the top of the bucket hanging on the side of the wagon, smashing straight into the box of caps that Denton had earlier fixed to the top of the keg of powder. The two-odd ounces of fulminate then exploded, setting off the five pounds of gunpowder. The result exceeded Jack Denton's wildest expectations.

From where he was crouched it looked to Denton as though an artillery shell had landed bang on the cart, so ferocious was the explosion. The wagon itself disintegrated in a flash of blue fire and cloud of sulphurous smoke. A moment later he felt a slight warm breeze on his face from the blast.

Most of the riders who had clustered round the wagon when the explosion took place had been either killed outright or gravely injured in the explosion. Only two men were still in the saddle and one of them was missing part of his right arm. The wagon itself had simply ceased to exist: blown to matchwood by the force of the blast. Denton set his musket against the wall and stood up, drawing his pistol as he did so. It would be unfortunate to be killed at this point, having achieved so much of what he had set out to do.

The only man who was more or less uninjured by Denton's mine was Carlos Mendez. His ears were ringing and he was in a state of confusion, but that was all. He looked around him in perplexity at the dead men and horses. The explosion had ripped open one of the chests of gold, scattering shining coins for yards around. As he tried to make some sense of what had happened Mendez became aware of an approaching figure. It was a man with a pistol in his hand and as he came closer he said, not to Mendez in particular but more as a general warning:

'Any man as draws on me, I'm goin' to shoot him down like a dog.'

Mendez's ears were still ringing from the explosion, but he heard clearly the warning and saw the pistol in the hand of the man walking towards him. He spoke to the young man: 'You intend to kill me as well?'

'If you're one o' them as snatched a little boy from his ma, then it's more'n likely,' said Denton casually. 'Games like that have a habit of ending badly.'

Carlos Mendez knew that unless he made his escape very soon he was liable to be lynched by the men of the town if they believed that he had been mixed up with child theft.

'As God is my judge,' he replied, 'I had no part of that. It was a private enterprise by a bunch of fools.'

Jack Denton's face was inscrutable, giving not the least indication of whether he believed this statement to be true. He simply stared impassively at the men on horseback. The injured one was groaning and staring disbelievingly at the ragged stump where his arm had once been. Mendez spoke again:

'Put up your weapon and give me a fair fight. You wouldn't gun down a man like this? I have no quarrel with you. But at least let us fight fairly, if fight we must.'

He couldn't have known it, but Mendez had touched a nerve in the other man. Denton knew fine well that he would not be able to shoot this man now, not without evening up the odds a little and letting the other man have a chance. It would have been another matter in the heat of battle, but he could not bring himself to kill a man with whom he had exchanged polite words in this way.

He toyed for a moment with letting this sole survivor just go free, but knew that this wouldn't answer. He had sworn a private oath that he would bring to book all those who had had a hand in taking Marion Fowler's child and here was surely one such individual.

'You got a choice,' he told Mendez. 'You can bide your time here and wait for the sheriff and his posse to return, or you can try conclusions with me this minute. It's up to you.'

'You'll give me the chance to draw?'

For the fraction of a second, Jack Denton was undecided. Then, realizing that in this man's place he would himself rather have risked his life in a duel than face certain death on the end of a rope at the hands of a court, he put up his weapon and returned the pistol to its holster to allow the rider to dismount and face him man to man.

The problem with decent and honourable men is that they are sadly prone to attributing a sense of honour to others even if, as in the present case, those men are the most unpromising of individuals. For all his wide experience of life on the plains and in some of the wickedest cities in the United States there was sometimes a touching naïvety about Denton, which was hard to credit in such a tough and capable man.

In the present instance he honestly trusted Mendez to climb down from his horse and then fight a fair gun battle with him, man to man. Matters did not quite work out in that way.

The Spaniard could scarcely believe his good fortune in encountering such a simpleton. He swung his leg over, preparatory to dismounting, and then, as he slid down, drew his piece. His back was to the man who stood there, waiting, and Denton could not, therefore, see what Mendez was about. Even if he could have done so, Mendez was pretty confident that here was not such a man as would shoot another in the back.

He felt a strange exhilaration. A few moments ago everything had been lost and he had thought to lose his life. It was true that the treasure, upon which he had expended so much energy and in pursuit of which much blood had been shed, was lost. Still, that was merely the fortune of war. It was sad but, when all was said and done, no worse really than losing a large sum of money at the faro table. At least he would live to fight another day.

The terrific explosion had alerted everybody in Jordan's Crossing to the fact that something terrible and untoward was happening in their town. Most sensible folk chose to stay in their homes and see how things turned out without their intervention. Others, such as old Mr Scott, had taken some action, even though it had proved to be directed at the wrong target. One man who was destined to play a crucial role as the events reached a climax that late afternoon was Charlie Culpepper.

Culpepper had been out doing business in a nearby mining camp and had missed all the excitement of the gang of bandits descending upon the town and seizing Mrs Fowler's store for reasons quite unknown. Just as he was riding back into Jordan's Crossing a tremendous explosion shook the ground, reminding Charlie Culpepper of his experiences in the war. He had been an artilleryman and the sound that he heard was exactly like the detonation of a five-pound shell.

On hearing Denton's mine being sprung Culpepper had apprehended immediately that something was amiss. He had dismounted, tethered his horse to a nearby hitching rail and then made his way cautiously to the site of the explosion, which was clearly indicated by a column of grey-blue smoke curling up into the sky. He arrived just in time to see the final act of Denton and Mendez's confrontation. Charlie Culpepper came up behind Mendez and had a clear view of the man on foot who was facing him. He recognized Denton at once as the man who had rescued Marion Fowler's boy after he had been snatched from his home.

Seeing Jack Denton, whom everybody in town knew to be a good man, told Culpepper all that he needed to know about the current situation, which was that Denton was squaring up to somebody who was probably some kind of criminal. It did not escape Culpepper's notice that the scene was littered with dead men and he assumed that Denton was about to disarm the man who was now climbing down from his horse. He noticed that Denton's gun was still in its holster.

Charlie Culpepper was the only eyewitness to what happened next, the explosion of the wagon having taken place just beyond the edge of town, where nobody cowering in their house and looking from the window would have been able to get a clear view of what was going on. As the man dismounted Culpepper watched in disgust as he drew his pistol and then, as soon as his feet were on the ground, whirled round and shot down Jack Denton, who was standing there without a weapon in his hand. Incensed at this crafty and underhand piece of work, Culpepper drew his own piece and shot the cowardly assassin in the back of the head. Then he ran to see if there was anything to be done for Denton.

Everybody in Jordan's Crossing had been enormously impressed with the neat way in which Jack Denton had rescued Davy Fowler and there wasn't a one of them who wouldn't have been glad to go to his aid. His stock was high in the town. So Charlie Culpepper was delighted to find that the man was only wounded. The ball had taken him in the shoulder, tearing through the chest muscles just below his armpit. It was messy and there was a deal of blood, but the injury didn't look to be a mortal one.

'Hoo, you're bleedin' like a stuck hog there, boy,' Culpepper said. 'Let's get you fixed up.' Then something shiny caught his attention and he added: 'You drop a gold piece?' He bent down to pick it up and then realized that the roadway was strewn with gold coins.

Slowly a trickle of people arrived at

the scene of all the action. Denton was aware of them but felt somehow unequal to the task of standing up and explaining what he had been about. It is a rare man who can be shot twice in a matter of an hour or so and still be capable of conducting himself as usual. Jack Denton simply felt tired and weak from loss of blood and he knew that if he stood up and moved around he was likely to faint. He was confident that somebody would see about fetching a doctor to him if he just waited patiently.

It took a while to locate Dr Carter, who had gone to tend to somebody on a nearby farm. Somebody rode out to fetch him as a matter of urgency, it looking to more than one bystander as though Jack Denton would not be long for this world if his wound wasn't properly bound up soon. By the time that Dr Carter got there it was twilight and Denton had lapsed into a pleasant state between consciousness and sleep. He was so far out of things that he was barely aware of Marion Fowler mopping his face and murmuring encouraging words to him.

Near by, her son Davy stared stonily at the gravely injured man.

11

As Dr Carter was tending to Jack Denton and dressing his shoulder there came a thundering of hoofs and the posse rode in. They had galloped hell for leather and would have broken records on the racetrack had there been any timekeeper. The knowledge that their wives and children were in a town undefended by the forces of law and order while a maurading gang of bandits was ransacking the place was a powerful incentive for them to get back to Jordan's Crossing as soon as ever they could.

Sheriff Quinn was not overly pleased to find that this rootless drifter, with whom he had already crossed swords, had perpetrated what was, to all appearances, a massacre; right on the very edge of town. It took only a few exchanges with those standing around to confirm what Quinn suspected, which was that Denton had been at the heart of the events which led to this grisly scene.

Public feeling, however, was very much in favour of Jack Denton; it would have been impolitic for the sheriff to castigate the man now, as he lay there helpless and covered in blood. Quinn restricted himself to observing to his deputy:

'Didn't I tell you that there was a man who brought down the lightning?'

It had not escaped notice that gold coins had been scattered far and wide by the explosion. Some of those who had gathered to see what was happening had been gathering up what they could of the treasure, so that it could be handed over to Quinn and his men. Incredible to relate, every last one of the gold pieces was retrieved and handed over to the authorities. Not one of the men collecting up those coins felt that it would be fitting or decent to loot the scene of so many deaths.

While all this was happening the man who had had his arm blown off obliged everybody by falling from his horse and expiring quietly from loss of blood and also internal injuries caused by the explosion.

Tidying away a bunch of corpses presented no sort of difficulty to Sheriff Quinn, neither did discouraging Charlie Culpepper from bragging about his own role in the business. As far as Quinn could see, the neatest way of accounting for this officially would be if Jack Denton had had a gunfight with the dead men and had killed them all, suffering injuries himself in the process. There was no call to start taking statements from anybody else claiming to have shot any of the bandits. Culpepper, who had been afeared that he might be charged with murder, was only too happy to have his part in the thing brushed under the carpet and he scuttled off home thankfully.

There remained the problem of what to do with the wounded man. This was

221

solved in the simplest way imaginable. Marion Fowler came up and tugged at the sheriff's sleeve.

'Would you think me forward, Sheriff, if I was to ask for help in getting that poor man to my place?' she said. 'I got a spare room where he could lay and I'd be honoured to tend him.'

'Why, that's right good of you, Mrs Fowler,' replied Quinn, exulting privately at seeing a tricky situation resolving itself in this way. 'If you're sure, then I'll fix up for a cart to take Denton — Mister Denton, I should say, to your house. Doctor's fees and so on'll be billed to the town, naturally.'

There was something else causing concern to the Widow Fowler, who carried on standing before him, looking a little embarrassed.

'Was there something more?' asked the sheriff.

'You'll think me a greedy wretch, Mr Quinn, but from what I hear that gold was dug up from under my store. D'you suppose that there'll be a finder's fee or reward or anything of that kind?'

Sheriff Quinn looked at the pretty young widow in surprise. He wouldn't have thought that she was the type to even think of such a thing.

'Well now,' he said slowly, 'that's an interesting point. I shouldn't be at all surprised to learn that you might be right about that, Mrs Fowler. You have a lease on the store, don't you? Happen that would mean sharing any reward with the man who actually owns the place. But I'd say you should be in line for something.'

'I wouldn't have asked, but truth to tell, I'm finding it a bit of a struggle right now . . . '

'I'll engage to look into it for you and let you know what I find out.

After Denton had been carted away to Mrs Fowler's house and the various corpses and bits of corpses had been collected and stored in an old barn, Quinn took stock of things and turned his attention to the gold. There were two iron-bound chests, which had presumably been carried on the wagon that had blown up. One of the boxes had split open and some of the contents were spread far and wide, but the other was intact. It was so heavy that the sheriff could not lift it unaided. He called to a passing man:

'Hey, lend a hand here and help me carry this over to the Royal Flush.'

The little casket had two handles, one at each end. When the other fellow helped pick it up, he whistled in surprise.

'What the Sam Hill you got in here, Sheriff?' he asked. 'Lead?'

'Something like that,' grunted Quinn noncommittally.

The barkeep at the Royal Flush was intrigued when Sheriff Quinn entered the premises and asked to use the scales that were used to weigh supplies as they were delivered. There had been a lot of cheating going on at one time and the owner of the Royal Flush concluded that the only way of putting a stop to the short measures he was being fobbed off with was to weigh all deliveries as they arrived at the back door.

Discovering that the small box weighed in at a shade over two hundredweight gave Quinn a bit of a shock, even though he'd known that it must have been something like that. If this box was, like the other, crammed with gold, it meant that he was dealing with . . . how much?

Sheriff Quinn wasn't exactly a whale at ciphering, but after some prolonged mental effort, accompanied by much head-scratching, he managed to multiply sixteen by fourteen and proceeded from there to a calculation that yielded the astounding figure of $160,000. Such a sum was beyond all imagining and for a moment he was struck with a sudden suspicion. Was this stuff real? What if this was some elaborate hoax that would end in making a fool of him?

As a first step he must get this box and the scattered contents of the other one under lock and key for the night. It was true that people had acted honestly so far, but $160,000 was the hell of a lot of money and Sheriff Quinn had seen murder committed for a thousandth of that amount.

When he came round the next day Jack Denton couldn't for the life of him work out where he was or what had happened to him. He had a vague recollection of the explosion and of being shot afterwards, but subsequent events were hazy in the extreme. He looked around in bewilderment. He appeared to be in a comfortable bed in what looked to be a private house. On the wall opposite was a mezzotint of the Holy Family on the flight into Egypt, and on the table next to the bed was a Bible; both these suggested that the owner of the house was a God-fearing individual.

He could only assume that he had been brought here to recuperate after the shooting. While he was mulling this over the door opened and in walked Marion Fowler.

'Oh, you're awake now,' said Mrs

Fowler. 'Could you manage a bowl of soup? Dr Carter said to give you something light to eat as soon as you felt like it.'

'How long have I been asleep?'

'Let's see, it's nigh on eleven now and you were fetched here at about seven last night. Maybe fifteen or sixteen hours, I guess.'

Denton thought for a moment and then asked:

'What condition did those rascals leave your store in, ma'am?'

There was to Marion Fowler something ineffably touching about the fact that this man, who had very nearly given his life on two separate occasions in the defence of her interests, should be chiefly concerned now with the state of her little store.

'Well Mr Denton,' she said lightly, 'those fellows weren't the neatest of workmen and I think that they were more concerned with getting the job done swiftly than with taking care of my property. I won't deceive you, it's in a pretty fine mess.'

'I'm sorry to hear it. Maybe when I'm recovered a little I shall be able to help tidy it up some for you.'

Marion Fowler shook her head firmly.

'You done enough for me and mine to last a lifetime, Mr Denton,' she replied. 'I can't ever repay you, but I don't aim for to take any further advantage of your good nature.'

A few hours later, after Denton had had a bite to eat and dozed a little, Sheriff Quinn called by to visit him and also to convey some news to the woman of the house. Quinn knocked on the door of the room where Jack Denton was tucked up in bed.

'Come in,' said Denton, wondering who this could be. When he saw who it was he added, in a less than welcoming voice, 'Oh, it's you, Sheriff.'

'Yes, large as life and twice as natural,' said Quinn, in a more jovial way than Denton had yet heard him speak, 'How are you doing?'

'Fair to middling. To what do I owe this pleasure?'

'Dropped by to tell you that all the witnesses agree that you acted honourable and that I've no intention of indicting you for murder or aught like that. Thought you might o' been anxious.'

'Not hardly. I saved you a heap of trouble.'

'Well, well, that's as maybe. Could be that there's a bounty on one or two of them boys you killed. It'll need to be confirmed, but if so, then the money's yours.'

Denton thought this over and then said: 'What about Mrs Fowler? She get that gold as was found 'neath her store?'

'Belongs to the government. She'll get ten per cent reward, have to split it with the fellow who owns the land her store's sited on.'

'How much'll she get?' asked Denton curiously.

'Something like eight thousand dollars,' was the surprising reply.

After Quinn had left, with various conventional expressions of goodwill and hopes for Denton's speedy recovery, Jack Denton thought hard about what he had now learned. It seemed likely that, through his efforts, Marion Fowler was now financially secure; not only that, but he himself might be in line for some cash money as well. Although this had not been his primary motive in acting as he had done, surely this sudden windfall would have the effect of inclining Marion Fowler favourably towards his suit?

Having nothing else to do as he lay there, Denton, who was not in general given to daydreaming or thinking of plans for the future, began to construct a pleasant future for himself which entailed him and Mrs Fowler marrying and perhaps setting up on a little homestead together. He was in any case, as a veteran, entitled to a grant of 160 acres of land under the Homesteader's Act, but up to now he had never seen the point in claiming it.

Gradually, as he recovered, this fantasy became stronger and stronger, until Denton had more than half-persuaded himself that he was capable of realizing his dreams. It was in this optimistic frame of mind that, a week after being shot, Jack Denton was fit enough to get dressed and take a short turn up and down Main Street.

Denton's progress along the town's chief thoroughfare was a slow one, for every person he met insisted upon shaking his hand and congratulating him upon his exploits. He was quite exhausted by the time he returned to the house where he was staying. While convalescing he had made a firm and determined resolution to ask Mrs Fowler to be his wife, just as soon as he was able to move about unaided once more. That time had come and, despite his nervousness, he intended to enter her house and make a declaration of love to her: the first woman to touch his heart since the death of his wife and child all those years ago.

There was a horse tethered outside the Fowler house when Denton returned from his little perambulation. Callers were not a frequent occurrence at Mrs Fowler's place and he wondered who this could be. It didn't take long to find out. When he entered the kitchen Denton found a blue-coated cavalry officer sitting at his ease, engaged in an animated and lively conversation with Marion Fowler. They gave every impression of being old acquaintances. When the stranger saw Denton he jumped to his feet, a broad smile upon his good-natured face.

'Mr Denton,' he said, 'I've been hearing so much about you. I'm eternally in your debt for what you've done for Marion and Davy.'

There was to Denton's ear something horribly familiar in that casual use of Mrs Fowler's Christian name, something that boded ill. So it proved, because his worst fears were realized when Marion Fowler herself said: 'Mr Denton, I'd like you to know Captain McCall. He's my fiancé.'

'Your fiancé?' asked Denton, stupefied.

'Yes, we hope to be married this fall.'

The soldier joined in at this point, saying: 'I been away for a while and come back to find all hell — I beg your pardon, Marion — I mean that all sorts of things have taken place. From all that I'm able to apprehend you've stood friend to Marion throughout it all. I'm mighty obliged to you.'

Jack Denton shrugged diffidently. Already that absurd dream of him marrying a woman like Marion Fowler had vanished like the morning dew. It wasn't to be thought of and had never been a practical plan.

'Glad to know you, Captain,' he replied. 'I can leave town now, easy in the knowledge that somebody's looking after Mrs Fowler here's interests.'

'Oh, you're not fixing to leave yet awhile surely, Mr Denton?' asked Captain McCall's fiancée, 'I was hoping that you'd plans to settle hereabouts.'

'Me? Settle?' asked Denton, with a

faint smile playing about his lips. 'I don't think it for a moment, ma'am. Maybe I'll be back in these parts again some time and I can look in on you and your husband, as he's like to be by that time. You and the captain'll forgive me, I got to step out again. Something I quite forgot while I was out.'

When Denton walked into Sheriff Quinn's office, Quinn greeted him by saying:

'You look like hell! Shouldn't you still be in bed?'

'What are you?' growled Denton. 'A sawbones as well as a sheriff? Any objection to me leaving town?'

'None that I'm aware of. When you fixin' to go?'

'Right now,' was the surprising answer.

Although he'd wanted to be rid of this troublesome stranger for a while now, Quinn felt a little sorry at the thought of the man just slipping away like this.

'There was talk of having some kind

of party at the Royal Flush when you were up and about,' he said. 'To thank you, you know.'

'Sounds just awful,' replied Denton, with deep and sincere feeling. 'I never could abide a fuss. You got that saddle of mine back there?'

'Surely. You want it now?'

'Yes, please. I see that rifle and scattergun of mine there, too. I'm obliged to you for looking after 'em. I'll take them as well.'

As he handed over Denton's belongings the sheriff looked hard at the man, who was still exceedingly pale and looked as though he really ought to be resting up.

'What about any reward money on those men as you killed?' he asked.

'I'll write you. I suppose you can send it on? What's it amount to?'

'If I'm right, about eight hundred dollars. Sure, I can forward it. You surely earned that cash.'

Now that it came to the point Sheriff Quinn was strangely reluctant to bid farewell to the man.

'You're a hard study, Denton,' he said. 'A man who's not easy to figure out. You never feel like settlin' down in one place, 'stead o' wandering all the time?'

'Me? Settle down and marry and such? Not hardly.'

'Well then, I guess I'll say goodbye,' said Quinn. The two men gripped each other's hands, then Denton was gone, striding down the street with his saddle balanced on his shoulder and the rifle and shotgun clutched in his hands.

We do hope that you have enjoyed reading this large print book.

Did you know that all of our titles are available for purchase?

We publish a wide range of high quality large print books including:
**Romances, Mysteries, Classics
General Fiction
Non Fiction and Westerns**

Special interest titles available in large print are:
**The Little Oxford Dictionary
Music Book, Song Book
Hymn Book, Service Book**

Also available from us courtesy of Oxford University Press:
**Young Readers' Dictionary
(large print edition)
Young Readers' Thesaurus
(large print edition)**

For further information or a free brochure, please contact us at:
**Ulverscroft Large Print Books Ltd.,
The Green, Bradgate Road, Anstey,
Leicester, LE7 7FU, England.
Tel:** (00 44) **0116 236 4325
Fax:** (00 44) **0116 234 0205**

CHISHOLM TRAIL
SHOWDOWN

Jack Tregarth

For the young men in the Texas town of Indian Falls, riding the Chisholm Trail as cowboys is a rite of passage. Dan Lewis is heartbroken when it looks as though he is to be cheated of his chance. Determinedly, he manages to secure a place on the trail, but his joy quickly fades as he is accused of cattle rustling and nearly lynched. As he fights to clear his name, he finds himself up against a gang of the most ruthless men in the state . . .

LAND OF THE SAINTS

Jay Clanton

It is the summer of 1858, and the Turner family are making their way along the Oregon Trail to California. The wagon train with which they are travelling is attacked by a band of Paiute, but this is no mere skirmish in the Indian Wars. The territory of Utah, or Deseret as those who live there call it, is in open rebellion against the government in Washington. Turner and his wife and daughter are caught in the crossfire of what is turning out to be a regular shooting war.

FLAME ACROSS THE LAND

Colin Bainbridge

Fark Seaton comes to the aid of old timer Utah Red when he and his flock of sheep are attacked. Who is responsible? The evidence seems to point towards Mitch Montgomery and his Lazy Ladder outfit; but as tension mounts and the bullets fly, Seaton is not so sure. What is the role of Nash Brandon, owner of the Mill Iron? Could Seaton's interest in Montgomery's daughter, Maisie, be clouding his judgement? When the sparks of anger finally blaze into uncontrolled fury, the answers at last begin to emerge.

TO RIDE THE SAVAGE HILLS

Neil Hunter

Arizona, 1888: Marshal Ed Pruitt had been bringing Sam Trask to justice when, following an accident, Trask murdered the driver and escaped. Now Pruitt wants Bodie to bring Trask in before the wanted man can cross the line into Canada. But what should be a straightforward pursuit soon turns into something far more puzzling. Trask is a killer, yet people are willing to cover for him. As he rides the savage hills, facing bullets and treacherous weather, Bodie proves that he's the toughest manhunter the West will ever see . . .

A GUN FOR SHELBY

Jake Henry

1867 and the Civil War was still being fought . . . Forced into taking a job he doesn't want, Savage rides into a desert full of hostile Yavapai Indians to track down a killer. There he is taken captive by a small band of rebels for whom the Civil War has never ended. Although their leader, the legendary General Jo Shelby, now wants to return to Missouri, some under his command would rather see him dead than betray their cause. Can Savage get Shelby home in one piece before the desert is wrenched apart by the explosive fury of the Yavapais?